T0065571

WHISPERS UNDER THE SUN

WHISPERS UNDER THE SUN

A Collection of Short Stories

ANUBHA SAGAR

PARTRIDGE

To order additional copies of this book, contact
Partridge India
000 800 10062 62
orders.india@partridgepublishing.com

www.partridgepublishing.com/india

CONTENTS

FOREWORD

This book in your hands is written by a sixteen year old girl. It is a compilation of exciting and spell binding short stories from a wide variety of experiences in our life. Good writing is not common to find and starting at such a young age is a primer for greater work in the future. "Whispers Under the Sun" is the second book by Anubha Sagar, which has come close on heels after her first book "The Journey of Deceit", which she penned at the age of fourteen years.

A reading child is often a successful child. This should not be a surprise, because those who read often open up new worlds and take on new journeys in life. There are many people who read, but the one who pens down his or her thoughts is the one who shows a glimpse of the new worlds to others. They embark on the most epic of voyages and explore their own identities and imagination deep inside themselves. A young mind is often more pure to begin with and has a fertile imagination.

In my decades of experience as an academician, this is a rare occasion when I have come across a talent and flair for expression, penned so well. Each story kept me glued to the book waiting for more. The varieties of ideas, depth of emotions and humour have been expressed well. The stories in the book have a seamless flow of thoughts with a teenage view of the world, embroidered neatly where required accompanied by the right emotional pitch.

I am proud of the fact that Anubha is a student at my school. I am sure that "Whispers Under the Sun" will be a gateway to success in her long career ahead. I wish the readers a pleasurable reading.

Yours sincerely

Harinder S Mann
Director
Doon International School
Dehradun

1

THE ROYAL SAFARI

The grass was tall. Very tall and was above our heights. It was called the elephant grass. The ground was slushy at places. It rained two days ago. There was a faint scent in the air of fresh rains. The Sun was blazing warm, though it was still the morning hours. The bush was thick and few mosquitoes and other insects could be seen flying in clusters. A swarm of locusts had just past the area three days ago. Some nearby agricultural fields had simply vanished in thin air. Overall it was a lazy morning, but sweaty. Our family sweated with difficulty, a genetic problem but could manage well in shade. I trotted with my mother across the bush. We were walking through on a semi beaten track. A herd of elephants had crossed and treaded on this path in the morning. The dung was fresh. We avoided wading into it. It was thick and high.

We didn't speak for some time. Our father had left us some days ago in search of better dwelling. We received a message from him yesterday that he had found some areas deep in Kaziranga where life is comfortable. The pigeons

The grass was tall. The ground was slushy due to recent rains.

had brought the message, yes the very old way. We still continue to live the old fashioned way. We don't have access to modern technology and money. Barter system and defence of grazing land remains our food security.

We had to walk the whole day and would probably reach the deeper parts of the forest reserve by evening. We had to make it before sunset. There are snakes and predators in the forest. Though men have killed off most of the predators, some have survived thanks to the government's conservation measures. Of course there may be some unfriendly rhinos on the way, but we will not make eye contact with them. They will not feel threatened and will let us pass.

"Ma, I heard that some foreigners of royal origin from a far off land are coming to Kaziranga today", I said. Daksha kept on walking behind me and said, "Yes, Prince William, the duke of Cambridge and his wife Princess Catherine Middleton, the duchess of Cambridge are in town. They must already be in Kaziranga." I got excited and turned back, "How does the princess look like? Is she beautiful?" I asked. Daksha my mother looked at me lovingly and said, "Gorma, you are so beautiful. Nobody can be more than you." I turned ahead and happily trotted across the trail carefully avoiding the dung. Wow, I was beautiful like a princess! We don't have a mirror at home. I hardly looked at my reflection except at the river and that too gets distorted when I touch the water. Most men consider us to be very poor since we have almost no worldly possessions. Our only claim to fame amongst the community we live in is that we have NRI (non resident Indian) relatives in Africa, Sumatra and Java, whom we have never met or spoken to. They are only folklore tales to spruce up our life. The African relatives I am told are fair and whiter than us. The government I believe has provided our community with a lot of funding, facilities and protection from the "haves" of the society but we still roam around this forest in the same way as our ancestors used to do many generations ago, in the open, exposed to the elements and vulnerable to all. Some of my friends and relatives died last monsoon in the flooding of Kaziranga and Pobitra forests.

"Ma, can I meet Kate the princess?" I asked. "No. Royal people decide whom they want to meet. You can't meet them by your choice. You can put up a request. They may accede to it if they want," Ma said. "But the same is true in democracy too. I can't meet the prime minister or the chief minister. Then how is democracy different from aristocracy?" I had asked a seemingly very intelligent question. Ma always said that I don't ask intelligent questions. I must read more and stimulate my intellect. "Work to attain such a stature that people seek to meet you. That is progress. But I know the way you are growing and maturing one day you will be a prominent personality Gorma and people will line up just to have a glimpse of you," said Daksha. How will that happen? We are so poor and live in a jungle. We are barely able to meet our food and shelter requirements. We don't eat meat, rather can't afford to have it. People will queue up to meet me? Unlikely, I thought. Even if yes, then how? And when? "Ma, why don't we eat meat? Many of my friends have it. We can't afford it, right?" I asked on seeing the carcass of a wild boar on the way. "Have you seen the way our family puts on weight? It is in our genes. Family problem. We eat only vegetarian food, walk all day long, yet put on weight. If we eat meat we will swell up. That is why," Daksha said.

I knew she was lying. She was trying to conceal the fact that we are poor. Surely we could have it once.

A helicopter passed over us. It was the security for the royal couple. The sound scared me. The bushes went flat. We became vulnerable to predators. Fortunately there was no dust as the ground was still wet from the rains, few days ago. We went on. Some flies were buzzing around the dung. They were a nuisance. I said "Ma, these flies are a nuisance." She said, "God created flies in his wisdom but forgot to tell us why." I was bemused at her reply. It was a rare occasion that she would be in a humorous mood. As we moved on I saw a dead fox, all skinned and the carcass lying in the bushes. Some vultures were hovering around. "Why, remove the fur and leave the animal. Why kill if you don't want to eat? Who killed it? Predators would have eaten it." Daksha replied, "It takes forty dumb animals to make a fur coat but only one to wear it. *All animals except man, know that the main aim of life is to enjoy and they do it as much as man and other circumstances may allow*" with tears in her eyes. Profound indeed. I had heard this before. "Ma, which is your favorite animal?" I asked. Daksha quipped, "As Churchill once said, I am fond of pigs. Dogs look up to us. Cats look down on us. Pigs treat us as equals." I loved the swings in the serious and humorous notes in my mother.

We had to cross a stream. There wasn't much water in it. We just needed to wade across. Just as we reached the other bank, I notice a long grey stone like structure. It was a statue. I noticed that it had a pretty long face and head with jaws open. Just then it moved. "Ma, Lacoste!!" I said. "No silly, it is called a crocodile!" she replied quietly. She knew that I was picking up the one liner punch sentences from her. I was proud of my sense of humor and continued walking with my head high. "Ma let us play a quiz game. We can pass time as we walk." "Ok shoot," said Daksha. "How can you drop a raw egg on a hard concrete floor without cracking it?" I asked. "Concrete floors are hard to crack. And definitely not with an egg!" said Daksha. "How many birthdays does an average French woman have?" asked Daksha. "Only one. Rest are all anniversaries" I said. "Hmm, great" Daksha said. I asked "What happened when the gun was invented?" "Man became an animal...." her voice trailed off. "*Down! Down! I say down!*" cried Daksha in a sense of hurry.

We saw through the bushes. What we saw was horror. There was a small clearing in the jungle. My uncle Mahanta was lying dead on the ground. Four dirty looking men had just sawed off his face. He was bleeding from the nose. He lay motionless, bleeding profusely. He was almost dead. No body movements. One of the men had a rifle and one had a saw. The third had a machete. Daksha was seething with anger. She rose up and snorted. And within three seconds I could see her charging towards the men. Before they knew the man with the machete was high in the air. Daksha's horn had pierced his back. As he fell I could hear a loud crack of his skull. He lay motionless. Quickly, Daksha turned to the man with the saw. I had never seen her so furious. She was all over him. The man with the rifle managed to run a few scores of feet away from Daksha and had trained his rifle at her. Daksha meanwhile was quick to turn. And pretty fast she turned for a rhino. The man fired. Daksha took a hit on the shoulder, but what is a single bullet for the thick skinned we are. She charged at him unfazed. Within seconds her horn was deep in his belly and he was hung on Daksha's head. With a swing she threw him down and trampled upon him. That was the end of him. The fourth man was running towards me. I suddenly stood up and blocked his path. I was no baby rhino. I too was about six hundred kilograms by now. Before he realized, he had hit me head on, and he fell down prostrate. I just walked over him and closed the chapter.

Mahanta was lying motionless. The horn was lying few feet away. He had been shot eight times in the belly. Daksha went close to Mahanta and sniffed him. I gently nudged his ears. Mahanta opened his eyes. The eyes had a forlorn look. They were gazing at infinity. His empty eyes briefly met Daksha's wet eyes. He blinked his eyelids twice as if to thank her and then they closed forever. One more of our community was gone. So much so for the security for the royal couple. Poaching had happened right when they were there in Kaziranga. It was a slap on the face of the government and *Operation Rhino*.

Sometimes I wonder whether man should be classified as a beast. Amongst all beings in the animal world, man is the only predator who kills for fun or for trade in animal parts. Man is the only beast who kills his own type also, not only for territory but for other emotions and greed. All other animals will kill for survival. Mostly they will scare away the other animal out of their territory and injure at the most. Once out of their territory they will quit the chase. But man's greed and merciless behavior knows no boundaries. For their own problems they have human rights but animal rights are for lip service only. Millions of animals are killed at the abattoir every day to stimulate their taste buds but if one man is killed by an animal then it is called a man eater. Rhino horns are an aphrodisiac? Come on, give me a break. Men are six billion and we are just few thousands and they say that we harbor aphrodisiac? It should be the other way round. Men should be crushed and fed to us. We need an aphrodisiac to increase our numbers! Did God actually create this divide? Food chain hierarchy is part of nature and is acceptable. But why is extra constitutional extra natural being called man? When every fish is killed, every river is polluted, every animal is killed and all trees are felled then he will realize that he cannot eat money.

Daksha and I moved on to the lands of better pastures where my dad was waiting. Life will continue till we will be extinct and future generation will put up our fossils minus the horn in museums.

2

A PALM SO SOFT

The clock ticked eight in the evening. The Saxena family entered its house after a two hour cultural program. It had been Eva Saxena, their daughter's school annual function.

"Excellent Eva! Keep working hard this way. I'm sure that one day you *will* reach your ne plus ultra," said Mr. Saxena, exuberantly. Mrs. Saxena, although highly elated, for her daughter had bagged prizes and had been awarded for being the most efficient student in school, masked her feelings. She didn't want to cry in front of her daughter, even though hers would have been tears of joy.

Eva, happy as she was, walked straight into her room. After turning the lights on, she opened the lid of her laptop and turned some music on. 'Life's good…God's great' she thought.

Bolting the door from inside, she paced towards the bathroom. With the twist of the tap's knob, gushed down fresh, cool water that Eva splashed onto her superfluously make-up covered visage, courtesy the annual function.

The rouge and foundation smoothly trickled down her cheeks, caressing the chin and then falling off its edge, marking the culmination of the annual function.

Putting on a pajama and a loose T-shirt, she picked her laptop up, hopped onto her bed and curled up in the blanket. Propped up on a few pillows, she clicked open her Facebook account.

Laudatory messages had inundated her inbox. So many notifications, a few friend requests and a series of messages had all piled up, waiting to be seen and read. After addressing all the notifications and replying to all the messages, she finally viewed the friend requests. Lots of people whom she'd met during the rehearsals of the annual function had sent her friend requests. There were three people whom she didn't know, so naturally, she had to check their profiles.

"Who's this girl? Nope. Decline request….Ah, I know *this* girl, Avanti… Yes, accept request. Okay…I think I know this guy…yes, of course! He was there during the annual function…hmm…Arush Mishra," Eva muttered to herself.

"He's so handsome, absolutely wow…" continued Eva as she glared at Arush's profile picture.

Yes, Arush indeed was an Adonis. He was 16 and was aptly tall for his age. With a well-chiseled face, an idyllically molded nose and neat, sharp eyebrows, he was surely a guy to be charmed by. His side beard complemented his otherwise clear cheeks. And his hair, fluffy and perfectly combed, made him a guy to be coveted. His brown-merging to-black eyes reflected affability. Yet, there was one quality of him that outshone all others- a tinge of golden glow that his face was suffused with.

She accepted his friend request[#]. With the click of the Accept Button, began her story. She had started crushing on Arush.

* * *

The sky was perfused with shades of blue and pink. The evening was calm and serene. Down below, lay Eva and Arush under the shade of an enormous tree, in a grove. Arush gently nudged Eva and held her hand.

A sudden flow on energy took place. Arush's hand in contact with Eva's had completed some sort of circuit. The energy exploded in Eva's veins. It gushed through the wriggly blood network, giving off sparks of joviality here and there and then, bombarded her heart.

The deluge of the humongous amount of energy sped up her heart beat. She tightened her grip on Arush's hand. But, why had his hand become so hard? She clutched her hand around Arush's, tighter still, yet it remained hard as wood…

* * *

[#]**Duh.**

"Eva, Eva!" someone screamed.

Eva sat up with a start. "Phew! Just another dream, that was," she said, feeling more relieved than ever. But, one thing was certain. Her hand was paining awfully. When she looked at it, she saw deep-red marks impressed on her palm. How they had come was no mystery. She figured out what she'd done last night. It was in the dream that she'd been holding Arush's hand. But actually, she had been holding the head rest of her bed.

Getting down from her bed, she walked across the room to the dressing table. She looked at herself in the mirror. Beads of sweat had formed an army on her forehead. The dream in particular had been a nerve-wrecking one, so sweating was quite justified.

"Eva! Come for breakfast," roared Mrs. Saxena.

"Yes, mum. I'm just getting ready".

It was the first day of the winter break. So, naturally, studies had been officially put aside. Eva got ready quickly and got her breakfast to her room. She sat down at her study table, keeping her laptop on it and began ogling at Arush's pictures on Facebook, as she gorged on the scrumptious breakfast.

After breakfast, she switched off her laptop and went to the kitchen to keep her plate. While coming back, she picked up the newspaper from the living room and walked out to the verandah to read it.

Having read the first page headlines, she was about to turn the page to some glamour news, when her eyes fell on a news snippet-

Famous artist Arush Gill to visit Pune for an art exhibition

Eva's heart skipped a beat. Now, it was just the name (Arush) that brought a smile across her face.

'Arush...oh dear...' she thought.

Eva's photo-watching business continued for four to five days until she'd gone through *all* of Arush's photos. She used to scroll down his Timeline, while her eyes met with multifarious photos; some which delighted her, some which she kept staring at and others that vexed her.

Arush's photos were an amalgamation of good and bad ones. 'Good' or 'Bad' wasn't in regard to the photo quality; it depended on the people in the photos. The photographs that had an equal proportion (or almost equal) of girls and boys, and the photographs that had only boys came in Eva's 'Good' category.

But, the photographs that had only girls or more girls and less boys, came in Eva's 'Bad' category. Too many girls standing with Arush irked Eva. Each time she came across a 'Bad' photo, the ire inside her head augmented.

When one constantly looks at another's photos, it is quite obvious to form opinions about that person. (*Especially, if the latter is the crush of the former.*)

So did Eva. For Eva, Arush was an extremely handsome, yet, down to earth person. His expressions were always calmly ebullient. From his many photos with his numerous friends, he surely seemed friendly and gregarious. And, the best part was that he didn't give the menacing smiles that most boys did.

Looking at him, one thing was certain- he didn't have a girlfriend. She somehow just felt it. And then, she believed in it. Arush was the guy for Eva. He was a guy for keeps. Their ages matched. Their complexions matched...well, almost. But, Eva and Arush were made for each other. As days passed, Eva's obsession-turned-love grew. She had all sorts of situations and their reactions framed in her head.

What if Eva met Arush in a book store? She had a reaction ready for that. And, what if they met at a party and got paired for a couple dance? She had a dance ready for that. She hadn't practiced the moves, but she knew them by heart. To any other person, this would've been a serious wastage of time. But, for Eva, this was the best way to utilize her time.

Time made headway. Then came the night of the 30th December 2014. Eva struck the date off on the calendar, with a marker. Tomorrow was a big day. After all it was New Year's Eve. The next morning, Eva woke up early and quickly got ready for the day. By 10 a.m., she was in the most expensive beauty parlor of the city. She got her hair straightened, her arms and legs waxed, eyebrows and upper-lip threaded and manicures-pedicures done.

She reached home at around 4 in the afternoon. After having few sandwiches, she rushed to the tailor to whom she's given her dress to alter. By 5:30, she was back home. She quickly slipped into her dress, wearing an expression of oh-I'm-looking-so-beautiful on her face. Then, she washed her face and dabbed on some foundation and rouge. Applying streaks of jet-black eyeliner along her lashes, she finally applied a shade of glimmering-pink lip gloss that complemented her overall appearance and made her look like a glamour diva.

Then, to get more publicity of her new look, she took a selfie and posted it on Facebook-#newyearnewlook.

Grabbing her favorite handbag and putting on three inch high stilettos, she sped towards her parents' room. "So, finally you're ready Eva. Let's go," said Mr. Saxena. In about ten minute's time, they reached the venue of the New Year Eve's party. "You surely take a whole day to get ready, Eva!" said Mrs. Saxena, as Mr. Saxena parked the car. "Yes of course…" said Eva, turning pink. Eva had to be embellished well. After all, Arush was coming to the party. Or at least, she believed he'd come, as most of the people from her school attended this party every year. So, why should Arush be an exception?

"Eva! You look so pretty," said Aishani, who was Eva's classmate and was looking gorgeous in a yellow dress, with a pink sash around her waist. "So do you Aishani!" said Eva, not completely paying attention. Her eyes were scanning the club for Arush. She waited for at least two hours, but there wasn't a sign of Arush anywhere.

When she'd lost all hope, a handsome face kindled the candle of joy in her heart. It was Arush! He was standing among a group of his friends. Many girls from Eva's batch (Eva, although Arush's age, was in a grade lower in school) went and wished Arush and his friends, but Eva... she just couldn't draw the guts up. Soon, the dance began. Eva was a natural dancer. And when she danced, all others paused to watch her breathtaking moves. During the dance, Eva saw Arush dancing...well, not quite openly, but then, he was dancing. Quite a few times, he cast his looks on her.

(Maybe he liked her).

She deliberately passed by his group to have a better view of him. All through the party, she didn't see him with any girl in particular. Now, she was sure that he didn't have a girlfriend.

From the next day, it was school again. Having scrutinized all off Arush's photos, she had identified his division. Eva wasn't the kind of girl who'd go around stalking people by literally following them tiptoe. Looking at photos was the limit. She didn't want to overstep and seem like a desperate lover, because she wasn't a desperate lover. True, she loved him ardently; she had no plans of telling him. She was happy just to know that he didn't have a girlfriend. She didn't want to tell him because of one simple and a very valid reason: she didn't want to get distracted during her studies. Besides, she felt complete in herself. She was happy just loving him (just that he should be single). So, at the base of things, she did want to tell him, but couldn't.

Slowly, she tried to convince herself with one thing- even if Arush did have a girlfriend, who didn't show up on New Year's Eve, it shouldn't affect Eva, because she hadn't confessed to Arush. This thought was a conflicting one. It constantly put her in a dilemma.

Finally, she sided with the opinion of not getting angry even if he did have a girlfriend, because, he was such a nice guy, that just like Eva, he would be more inclined towards his studies. So there was no scope of a girlfriend[#].

So, the problem was solved.

(But again, they were just conjectures).

Every week, the school choir, along with the school band, performed a song in the assembly. Eva waited eagerly for that day every week, since Arush was a member

---

[#]**Conjectures…so many conjectures.**

of the school band and he used to be up on the stage, performing.

Days went past. Arush often looked at Eva and made eye contact with her.

(Maybe he liked her).

Sometimes, when her luck sided with her, she got glimpses of Arush three to four times in a day. Sometimes, he jostled by her in a moving school crowd as well#. Life was beautiful for her. Time flew away slowly and steadily and Eva and Arush's silent love story (one-sided for now) continued.

Two years passed.

*   *   *

It was January 2017. The month was unusually gelid.

Some days into mid-January, the weather receded. Rays of hope of a warmer atmosphere returned. Eva, had come to eleventh grade and was about to enter twelfth in few months while Arush on the other hand, was in his twelfth grade, about to leave school in few months.

On January 27, Eva had to go to a party. So, when the day arrived, she planned her apparel in the morning. The party was indeed an enjoyable one. The tasty snacks, the savoury dinner and the delicious pudding made it worthwhile to attend the party. To add to the fun were

#**The feels!**

some games that she and the other people at the party played.

As Eva was talking to Romaa, the hosts' daughter, the topic of couples in the school came up. "There are so many couples in the school. If you sit down to enumerate them, you'd possibly take five days! said Romaa. "True, that is. I mean, there're umpteen couples in the school, all with their unique stories," said Eva, quite pleased with her knowledge. "Yes, especially the story of Arush and his girlfriend Richa," said Romaa, simultaneously texting someone.

Arush? Arush Mishra? Oh, definitely not. It couldn't be him. There were many boys in the school, with that name. *Arush Mishra* couldn't have a girlfriend. "Who Arush?" asked Eva, impatiently. "Arush Mishra, the handsome, brown eyed senior. He and his girlfriend Richa," said Romaa.

Eva's eyes became damp. She gulped her feelings down. "Are you sure?" she asked, getting jittery. "Yes, yes. Richa and he have been in a relationship for the past five years. And my word, what love! I've heard that they both love each other endlessly," said Romaa with great alacrity.

From that day, the usual charming smile on Eva's face started fading and slowly got replaced by a dark, glum scowl.

Eva had decided to tell Arush of her feelings for him. She *was* going to confess. And, that's when the biggest tragedy of her life struck like a bolt of lightning and burnt down all the happiness and enthusiasm in her. Now, with each passing day, the day when Arush would be leaving school, came closer.

Eva had had enough. She could no longer embed her love and bottle her feelings up. She decided to go and tell Arush of what she had in mind.

On February 23, something strange happened in school. "Eva! Have you heard? Arush Mishra, the senior, brown-eyed handsome guy…he says he wants to meet you. Now," screamed Aishani as she came rushing towards Eva and almost bumped into her. "Meet me?" said Eva, unable to digest the news.

"Yes, now go. He's waiting for you in the cafeteria".

"Okay, thanks".

"And remember one thing…"

"What?"

"It's the first time that you're going to talk to him, so…"

"So…what?"

"Look, I know how you've felt for him all these years. I saw it when you gave him those lovey-dovey looks. It was right there on your face. You're transparent. When you talk to him, make yourself opaque. Let him no see through you. If has something in mind, let him say it, okay?"

"Thanks Aishani!"

"Go now".

Aishani was almost sobbing. She knew. She'd sensed the ordeal that Eva had gone through.

Eva rushed down to the cafeteria and saw the guy to be charmed by- Arush.

She went to him, tapped his shoulder and said, "Uh, hi Arush".

"Hi Eva. Umm… come, sit here by me".

She sat on the soft-cushioned sofa, next to her Prince Charming. He held her hand and the circuit got completed. Love flowed through Eva's veins and bombarded her heart. But, this time, her heart didn't beat faster. Her heart, already beating fast, calmed down. It calmed down because Eva felt *complete*. Yes, she felt complete. Few years back, she may have felt complete *without* Arush, but now, she needed him to complete her.

She felt complete with Arush.

"Eva, you must be knowing about Richa and me…" said Arush, hesitantly.

"Yes, I do…" said Eva.

"But, you surely don't know that Richa and I…I mean, we met at Hyderabad Airport some days ago. And something didn't feel right. Although I had been with her since the past 5 years, I saw you in her eyes. And then, she told me that things weren't going on well between us, that's her and me. So, we called it quits.

I'm not a desperate, okay? I just love you. That's it".

Eva burst into tears. She got a feeling of compunction. She had wanted Arush to be single, but not at the cost of leaving his girlfriend. She felt as if she'd eyed their relationship ominously.

"Oh Eva! Don't cry. It isn't your fault. Don't believe in superstitions. Things had been rough for quite a while," said Arush, trying to pacify her.

"How…how do you know? How did you know what I was crying about?" she asked.

"You're innocent and transparent, Eva," he said.

Eva flung her arms around Arush and held on tightly to him.

"I…I love you too Arush!" she said, feeling happier than she ever had been.

"Yes, yes. I know dear. I mean, you gave me the 'Juliet' looks. Thought I wouldn't know?" he said.

*　　*　　*

The sky was flushed with dabs of magenta. The evening was soothing. Down below, lay Eva and Arush, hand in hand, in the shade of an enormous tree.

Their hands locked into one another's, Eva tightened her grip on Arush's palm.

This time, his palm was painless and soft, for, it wasn't a dream.

It was all so true.

3

EAST MET WEST

Aditi was getting married to Akash. The anointed day was 25 Oct 2015. There were still twenty days left. A lot of preparations were underway and some not even started. Hotel Green Emerald Delhi of the famous JJ group had been booked. It was a seven star hotel. Fifty rooms had been booked for 3 days, each at a handsome sum of rupees ten thousand per night. That was after concession. That was a neat one and half million rupees just for lodging. The dinner, decoration, other meals added up to another three million rupees. Guests were coming from all over the country and abroad. Aditi was waiting for her cousins Mrinal and Rohit. They would be arriving a few days before the marriage.

Aditi was an electronics engineer working at Bharat electronics Inc. She was the only daughter of her parents Mr and Mrs Singhania. Mr Singhania was a diamond merchant. Akash Subramaniam was also an electrical engineer working at Marson and Subre, a major infrastructure company. They had met at Chicago during the finalization of a joint project with the US on the building of nuclear power projects at India. They had been seeing each other for some time and were now engaged for the last two months.

Mr Gagandeep Singhania was a thorough businessman who knew his work well. It had been their family business in diamonds. Most of the work was outsourced from South Africa and Namibia to Surat, Gujarat and later, further distributed to good dependable traders. He was very rich no doubt. He paid his taxes, so he slept well. Mr Singhania was a very traditional and religious man. He had been educated at Harvard. He was a man of few words, but when he spoke, he talked sense. However he had his own issues in life. He did not approve inter caste, interstate marriages. He was against it but as luck would have it, he couldn't say no to Aditi's marriage to Akash. Akash was a Tamil Brahmin from Coimbatore. Aditi was too sweet and dear to him. Mr Chunnilal Devat Singhania, father of Gagandeep Singhania, was a wise ninety year old man. He was agile and active for his age. His day started at four thirty in the morning and after the morning chores he would go for a walk around the locality for an hour. A deeply religious man, he had contempt for everything that was western. He had a belief of superiority of the Indian culture and its history and was convinced that anything beyond twelve nautical miles of the territorial waters of India was generally inferior to India. Wonder if greater India had existed from Afghanistan, Pakistan, Bangladesh to Burma; then what would have been his views.

Mrs Singhania, Gagandeep's wife was more of a non entity as far as matters of say in the house were concerned. Though loved and respected by everyone, she rarely would air her opinions on anything and would agree with everything that Gagandeep said, something Aditi had decided very early in life that she would not do.

Aditi was, as expected, a modern girl, who had imbibed good aspects of Indian and western cultures. She was highly critical of some Indian beliefs, and at the same time she despised some features of the western culture as well. She was not always correct, though. There were serious gaps in her understanding of some Indian concepts. Akash too had similar views and thus went on well with Aditi. Mr and Mrs Subramanian were a middle class, educated couple. They were aware of other cultures like the north Indian culture, but weren't very glad to see their son adopting it. As all humans, they too had their bit of superstitions, but they kept it to themselves.

22 Oct 2015

Mrinal, Rohit and Catherine arrived in the Mercedes that Gagandeep had sent to the airport to receive them. Catherine was Aditi's friend, whom she met at a Himalayan trek and twice at business meetings in Germany and the

US. She was delighted to come for Aditi's marriage. She had to proceed to Singapore on 27 October for a business meet, so the dates suited her.

Mrinal and Rohit were brothers. They were both corporate lawyers and had their own law firm in the US. Aditi was delighted to see them. "Welcome, long time! Waiting to see all of you," said Aditi. Ramu Kaka, the Butler, ushered them to their rooms. Catherine too was staying with them. She was wearing a knee length blue skirt, a cream colored shirt with a black jacket and sandals to match. She was looking pretty indeed. She was around 25 years of age. She was engaged to Joe and was going to get married in Dec 2015.

When the three retired to their rooms to freshen up, Mr Singhania Sr quipped, "These western dresses are so cheaps. They reveal so much of skins. These people have no cultures," he said with an air of superiority. Aditi was close to her grandpa. Nobody could argue with grandpa except Aditi and often she would silence him and grandpa wouldn't mind. The only person who could make grandpa see reason was Aditi and no one else at home. "Grandpa, I have a question," said Aditi. "OK Shoots!" said the Sr Singhania. He was in a habit of using plurals unnecessarily. Initially it started as fun many years ago, but now it was part of his regular language especially when he was in discussion with Aditi. He knew English well. He had studied at Oxford. It was his quirk. "Grandpa what is preferable, showing off the tummy and navel, Seventy percent of your back and partial bosom or legs?" asked Aditi. "Preferably none," said grandpa. "OK, then is a saree more revealing or a skirt? What about the nine yard saree worn around in south central India? It also reveals legs. But no one objects. The regular saree also reveals ample tummy, back *and* extra bosom when the lady bends forward. Would you classify that as cheap?" "Hmm you got a points," said grandpa. "I never thoughts on those lines". "Grandpa, the bias is in the mind of the beholder and not dresses. If one views a woman as a sex object only then one would see the skin, but if you consider her as a person in whole then she is another individual who can contribute to the society just as men do," said Aditi. "Yes, agree. When are we meeting for a drinks before dinner?" grandpa said. "In another hour or so," said Aditi.

Catherine and Rohit were having red wine, grandpa was on scotch and Aditi and Mrinal decided to have sweet lime. Gagandeep was on Coke. He had to leave in the evening for an urgent meeting. "Ah, chicken tandoori, my favourite," Rohit exclaimed. "Have it. There are few days when non vegetarian food is permitted in Indian culture," said Aditi. "What do you mean?" asked grandpa. "See we have fifty two Tuesdays, twelve full moons, eighteen navratras, about ten more festivals in a year. Add to that some twenty to thirty days in a year when someone in the family decides to keep a fast on a Friday or a Monday.

That brings us to almost one hundred and twenty days a year when you don't have non vegetarian food in India if you follow the customs," said Aditi." "That works out to almost a third of a year," said Rohit. Everyone laughed except grandpa. "And pray have you thought why it is so?" asked grandpa. "Why?" asked Catherine getting interested because it was an entirely new concept to her. "Simple, superstitions," said Aditi. Gagandeep nodded his head in disapproval. "See in olden days many centuries ago, till about fifty years ago food was not as plenty as you would get now. Although, there are vast areas on earth even today where food is in shortage and famines do occur but that is due to the vested interests and mismatch of resources. Some countries like the US dumped wheat in the sea and in Ethiopia people went without food for years. It could have been passed on to the poorer countries. We are not talking about that. In those days food was actually less and entirely rain dependant, without technology, no pesticides or rodenticides and had low yield crops. Wars would result in burning of fields and granaries. Animals would provide milk and meat. But do you know that animals greenery many more times their weight and provide much less food in terms of meat. In addition they require time to grow and a lot of effort goes to take care of them. So meat was costly even then. In such a scenario people subsisted mainly on plant products and less on meat. It is possible that the concept of avoiding meat or food all together on certain days by means of fasting was a way to conserve food. Religious connotations were given and fear of God was instilled so that people would follow it. Besides, giving rest to the body and consuming lesser food maintains health and longevity. Look around the animal world. Many animals though not all, especially the carnivores do not feed every day. Vegetarian animals feed everyday and maybe all day long. Meat eating also brings to you all the unwanted toxins, chemicals and heavy metals that get deposited in bones, liver and other organs directly to your body. What the animal accumulated over a lifetime, you get in a single setting. It is possible that our ancestors understood this fact. History is written by the victors, and the first thing that is done when you win a country or culture, is to destroy their libraries and records and later replace it with your versions. So their scientific knowledge may have been destroyed over the years, but the customs continued. If you see around, Islam follows Ramazan fasting and Christians have the Lent. The great prophets of all religions must have had great wisdom and in addition to the religious connotation it is possible that these great men showed a path of food conservation too. What do you have to say on this?" said Grandpa. There was silence. Everyone was slowly allowing the information to sink in. "You have a great point sir," Catherine said. "Seems very logical," said Aditi feeling wise after grandpa's sermon. Grandpa gave the matter of fact look. "Maybe in process we became too much of vegetarian and became anti protein," grandpa said. "What is anti protein?" asked Rohit seeming interested. "Where is the protein in Indian diet? Milk and paneer is not consumed in sufficient quantities and pulses that most people consume are mainly water, principally diluted either as a matter of habit or due to poverty. Our foods are cereal based and potato based. Look at samosa, aloo parantha and aloo puri. We eat carbohydrate rolled up in another carbohydrate, deep fried. Rice with watery sambhar or dal, chapatti with veggies where potatoes are common ingredient!" said Gagandeep. Everyone was rolling in laughter. "In the west, diets are heavily meat based except for the poor. Bread, a refined carbohydrate is an accompaniment. They have their share of problems with obesity especially with fast foods becoming a fad. Pizzas loaded with extra cheese is only going to add up to your waist," said Gagandeep. "That means both the west and east have lopsided diets and both are obese due to different reasons, one with meat and fat and the other with carbohydrates and fat! Wow, I am glad I came here," said Catherine.

"When are the Gulatis and Sekhons coming?" asked Aditi. "They may not," said Gagandeep "Why??" asked Aditi and Mrinal almost together. "Relatives can be *painfuls* sometimes," laughed out grandpa. Singhania senior had seen a long life. "In the west, an invitation is an invitation. Earlier it was by a card, now card is getting replaced by email or sometimes both. They will acknowledge it and confirm if they can make it or not. No frills. But Indian relatives and friends are different," said Grandpa. "How?" asked Mrinal. Mrinal and Rohit had moved to the US as children and grew up there. They used to visit India once in a while and as expected did not know much about this place. "In north India, the custom is usually to go personally to give an invitation card at least to your closest relatives. It is generally accompanied with a packet or more of sweets or chocolates or fruits or all. Others too expect the same but the card must be delivered by some one. Sending by post is not considered polite. Courier is acceptable! Then on top of that you must request and plead in person, not once but many times. That should be followed up by few phone calls, reminder SMS and as the dates get close, more reminders. Arrange the stay and transport. Invite them on your facebook marriage page. If you falter in any one of these, there is a high chance that it will be perceived that the relatives are not wanted!" said Gagandeep. "Strange, but why?" exclaimed Rohit. "See traditionally, marriages were solemnized in front of a large number of kith and kin as a mark of proof that it had happened. Hence the importance of relatives and friends. But over the years all traditions get corrupted and people start getting the feeling that they are indispensible. Sad, but it is true. It is also true that the cycle of life and karma continues, we are just functionaries in it and no one, I repeat no one can stop a happening that is written in destiny. So if someone feels that he need not come, so be it. It is also true that when relatives do land up in marriages they have their 'requirements' and they may create a fuss. So it is good that such people are not coming," remarked grandpa. "Hmm, that was quite a new learning. Life would be much simple only if we could give up our egos for a while," said Catherine. "We need to learn a lot from each other. I learnt a lot of good things of India today and also saw some ways how things can get even better. I liked the food conservation part, reason for vegetarianism. I think we need to learn to conserve food. In our country people do waste a lot of food." she said. "And in India, we need to learn good work culture and ethics from the west and Japan in the east. They don't damage public property or go on strikes. That is just shooting your own foot. What started as a mark of protest against the British Empire to hurt *their* coffers has now been corrupted and now we hurt our own taxes and treasury. As a country we have to go a long way," said Gagandeep as he got up and excused himself. He had to go for the meeting. The others too had their meals and bade goodnight. It would be a long day ahead. Aditi, Rohit and Mrinal chatted for sometime before they retired to bed.

As Aditi lay on the bed, she was wondering how much she had learned in a span of an hour. East had met West. There was so much to learn and benefit from each other. She thought that she knew a lot. But today she realized that although she was well read, yet for wisdom and knowledge, there was still a long way to go. Why were they spending so much on the marriage? What a colossal waste! She had tried not to, but couldn't convince her parents. But one thing was certain: the marriage of her kids would be normal with no wastage. No more fat Indian weddings.

4

THE LAST THREE DISMAYS

There was something wrong with the cat, Maau. She was meowing louder than normal and was desperately trying to get inside our house. She was a community cat and I fed her. She was not allowed to get inside the house, although she did that quite often when no one was around.

After a while, she walked away. She came back after some time and seemed quite exhausted. She appeared somewhat different. She had become thinner, and the area around her stomach was wet. I went inside and got milk in a bowl for her. The pace, at which she lapped up the milk, was indeed remarkable. As Maau guzzled from the bowl, she spilled quite a few drops on the floor around. Each time, as she pushed her tongue back into her mouth, few droplets detoured and flew in the air... here and there, everywhere. After slurping to her fill, she sat down and looked extraordinarily at me. Her actions had puzzled me. After some time, she went away.

Sometime in the afternoon, she came back for food. I gave a half cooked egg to her. After gobbling it up, she rushed back hurriedly. Next morning too, she did the same thing. Her behavior was getting more ambiguous day by day. Her actions had stoked a strange urgency in me, and I decided to find out what the matter was. When she came for milk in the evening, I followed her and saw her climb up a tree. She jumped from the tree to the roof of our neighbor's garage and sat there, as though she were in a resplendent hall.

I couldn't climb it up and called out to my *Ayah*. She sent her son, who came with a ladder, all set to climb. He placed the ladder against the wall of the garage and climbed up. After reaching the top, he looked at me and grinned. I shouted, 'What is it? Is Maau okay?' He shouted back, 'Maau is fine and so are the kittens!' I was shocked. Maau had given birth to kittens. I was getting eager to see them.

One night around nine, I was sitting in the verandah. There was a bamboo swing kept in the corner of the verandah. We never found a hook strong enough to fix it. It thus occupied a corner of the verandah. Suddenly, Maau came and started sniffing that area. She jumped around the swing and around that place. The next day, when I came back from school, mother shouted from inside the house, 'Maau has got the kittens!' I kept my bag quickly and went towards the swing. The kittens were very sweet indeed. I looked at them and tried to go close to them. They reciprocated... not sweetly though. Rather, they retaliated and I retreated. They looked at me as though I was the first non-cat species they had encountered. I tried to pick them up, but they ran away and crammed up in a corner. There were a total of three kittens.

Maau fed them every two hours. Her appetite had also increased because of lactation. Over a few days, the kittens came out of the swing enclosure. They attempted walking. It was the most comical sight I had ever seen. They couldn't walk properly, since their limbs were neither strong nor properly developed. They would keep their fore limbs forward and their hind limbs would slip across, as though the hind limbs were involuntarily doing a yoga split. Their paws were tiny and the claws were mildly hard.

Some days later, the kittens learnt how to walk properly…well, almost properly. They finally came out of the swing corner and roamed about in the verandah. They would climb the garden chairs and sit on the window sills. During nighttime, they would climb the tyres of the bicycles in the verandah, hop from there and grip the window sill with their claws and sit there. The mother cat protected her kittens against other cats. The other cats often came to attack the kittens, and possibly to kill them. Cats have a peculiar manner of defending themselves. A female cat comes to another female, always with an intention to attack, never to make friends or to roam in packs. Once, a dull grey coloured cat came to attack

Maau. Maau got her attack mode on. Her fur rose up instantaneously, as though she were a porcupine. Her thin tail widened because the fur on her tail spread. Her hump rose and she stood, ready to attack. She then moved forward and made unpleasant sounds, conversing with the other cat. The grey cat descended, slowly, as though she promised to come back again.

As the kittens grew up, their colors became more vibrant. They became very pretty indeed. The kittens were colored in beautiful shades. The first one, White Mischief, as the name suggests, was white in colour, and its tail seemed to have been dipped in grayish-green paint. As for the second part of the name, the kitten was very impish.

Mother had forbidden my brother and me from getting the kittens or Maau, inside the house. White Mischief was the one who loved entering the house, when the doors were left open in the morning. It would get inside my room and go under my bed, and because of the boxes and other things kept under the bed, she would get ample amount of space to fit itself in and hide there. I would then have to go after her for at least half an hour. Getting a glass of milk, I would stand in front of her and lure her. Eventually, she would start following me towards the door. Her mother was also one special creature. She would keep sitting at the door for almost half the day, meowing for milk, milk and more milk. So, when I would

White Mischief, Brown socks and Black Forest

lead White Mischief out of the house, Maau would be at the door and White Mischief would sniff and finally be out of the house.

The second one was golden-brown in colour. So I named him 'Brown Socks'. His legs were over covered with fur and were soft as muslin. Brown Socks was a lazy kitten. He wasn't very agile and stuck to Maau for most of the time. He kept quiet and maintained a very low profile.

The third one, Black Forest, was black and white. He was colored black on the back and white on the chest. His body were black and paws were white. He had a very atypical color combination on the face. The forehead and cheeks were black, whereas the area around the nose and mouth was white. One thing was common to all the three kittens: pink noses.

Time flew and the kittens grew up considerably. They had started going to the driveway and in the garden. One evening, I saw the cat standing next to an Ashoka tree in the garden. Two of her kittens were standing beside her. All three were glaring above into the branches of the tree. I looked carefully at the tree. I couldn't make out anything. I went closer to them. Standing there, I looked above, but saw nothing. Suddenly, White Mischief fell right onto my palms. 'Mew, mew!' cried the kitten as I looked into her jade colored eyes. She was utterly stupefied and looked at me as though I were her savior. She grabbed my shirt with her soft claws and refused to get down. I loosened her grip gently and put her down. She hopped back to her mother with great joy. The mother cat licked her kitten, showing the love and affection which she had for her children.

With the passage of time, the kittens became comfortable with me. They jumped around me, when I came to put milk in the bowls. Now, there were a total of two bowls. One bowl to be shared by two. And the bowls were filled with milk, up to the brim. Once to twice daily, they got eggs and at least once in a week, they also were given some meat and bones.

In some more days, the kittens started accompanying their mother to roam in the nearby areas. During one such trip, the cat left her kittens in the verandah. She went alone. When she came back, she had some weird looking creature with her. Well…it was a rat and that too, a big one. The kittens shared that feast with the mother. Finally, they had tasted flesh, real flesh. Earlier, rats had been a real nuisance. They invaded the roof, nooks and corners of the house. With the coming of the kittens, the cat became more frequent in getting the rats. Once, she even caught a bird. In the morning, when I stepped out to take in some fresh air, I was surrounded by feathers, yes *feathers*. There were feathers everywhere. And, the uglier part of the picture was, there was blood in some places. *Ayah* was quite furious at that sight, but she cleaned it up. She loved Maau very much because she too had a pet cat.

The kittens were not capable of hunting rats and birds, but they did hunt small insects. They were young and fresh and were curious to know about the world around.

Sometimes, it so happens that we expect everything to be completely okay. We never expect things to go wrong. It happens because too many good things come in at once. Like those kittens. They were the reason for my smile in the morning. They were the reason for my discussions. There is so much I learnt from them. Their love was unconditional. The utter innocence which they had in their eyes was unmatchable. They talked to me with those deep emotions embedded in their eyes. What happened to those innocent eyes and their words, is something I'm going to tell you. How life takes turns, and how nature can change the course of anybody's life.

It was a sunlit afternoon. Maau was sitting comfortably in the verandah, with all the three kittens beside her. She was suckling the young ones. I was sitting there, just next to Maau, watching those beautiful creations of nature. Then, I remembered that mother had given some work to me, so I went inside. Sometime later when I came out, Black Forest was missing. Maau was getting restless. I calmed her down. After putting her and the other two kittens to sleep, I sat down wondering where Black Forest could've gone. Something struck me then. Once earlier, he and Brown Socks had gone off for almost the entire day and had come back safe and sound.

The next day, in the afternoon, I heard a dog barking. I went outside to see what had happened. A very low pitched meow came from the place where the dog was standing. I rushed towards the place. The dog ran away. I stood there aghast. Bending down, I picked up the small, innocent Black Forest. He was injured, almost to die. I looked in his eyes. He looked into mine and clung to me. His warm body burned a human's cold soul. His heart was beating riotously. I put my hand on his chest and rubbed it. His heart beats went through my nerves and my heart started to beat speedily and harder, as if it had beat for the first time. He kept his paw on my palm, his claws trying to hold on. He scratched my palm and I hugged him. I felt our hearts beating together. In some seconds, the sun was before my eyes. The true heart had stopped beating and the cold carcass was lying still, very, very close to me.

For some days, the Maau family was sad and quiet. But, they got over it and moved on.

The dogs knew it very well, that there was more to the food. Dogs became a regular nuisance in our neighbourhood. They came in huge packs. My family, the neighbors and I tried to protect White Mischief and Brown Socks as much as we could. I took the kittens inside the house and kept them in a box. They had become big, so they tore open the box and I had to run after them. Maau also gave her best. She hid them somewhere for the afternoons and got them back in the evenings.

One morning, White Mischief was nowhere to be seen. Our neighbor came to us, walking steadily. She was gasping. She said something which broke my heart... maybe forever. White Mischief's body was lying in her garden, as she told, and the servant had removed it in the morning. White Mischief had been ripped apart by the dogs and was gone forever.

The kittens had spent so much time with me. And the dogs had taken it away in just a jiffy. Brown Socks caught my attention. I took utter care of him. I kept him inside the house at night. The slightest whine of the dogs was terror for the cats. One such day, I was washing my hands, when I heard a low whine. I speeded up. Washing my hands quickly, I rushed to the door. The cat and Brown

Socks had just finished their meal. I sat there next to them, because I sensed danger. After five minutes, there was a dog approaching the verandah. I ran towards him and chased him. On reaching the turning in the driveway, I saw a whole pack. I got even more furious. I ran after them, till they went off into a distance.

Brown Socks was maybe, not accepted by nature. One morning, a cat came. It wasn't just any cat. It was the grey cat. She had lived up to her promise, I suppose.

Maau and Brown Socks got in the attack form. The grey cat was very cunning and knavish. I was sure that my cat would defend herself, so I didn't meddle. The cats got into an actual skirmish. Brown Socks came rushing to me. I lifted him up. I didn't go to rescue the mother. I was scared that Brown Socks would get attacked. I fled and hid behind a pillar in the verandah, to watch the cats.

Hopes are not always realities. Maau got brutally injured. I had thought that the other cat would leave soon. Instead, she turned to me.

She advanced towards me and before I could do anything, she pounced on me. Brown Socks dropped from my hands. It was one swift stroke. Brown socks was lying motionless. The grey monster had vanished.

I stood there, helpless… watching as Maau carried the kitten into the mist. The fight was probably the nature's way of ensuring that only the strong seed survived and none else. I was wondering whether I should kill the grey cat to ensure the survival of Maau's next flock. But then I decided not to. I did not want to mess with nature. It was best left to Maau to fight things out.

Maau did have a new litter. But that is another story.

5

THE PREACHER

The day was balmy. The sun was dazzling through the white, cottony clouds ambling across the sky. There certainly was something novel about the day, something that got Ira Zariwala out of bed *early* on the very first day of the summer vacations.

Sliding the curtains, she let the sunlight transcend her room. She didn't know why she was excited. It was the sort of gut feeling one gets when everything is perfect in one's life.

Soon, having completed the routine chores of the morning, she stood before the mirror, her long fingers cajoling her face with a cream that assured 'Natural Glow'. Having applied it, she looked at herself for one last time in the mirror. Her short hair hung till her shoulders and her eyes, narrow and pitch black, had a strange glint. Her nose was small and pointed, while her forehead was covered by a curtain of fringes. Smiling for one last time at her reflection, she sped downstairs to the dining room.

"Good Morning, Ira," sang Mrs Zariwala.

"Good Morning, mother," said Ira, returning the greeting.

"I have some news for you, Ira," her mother said, curving her lips into a smirk.

"And what might that be?" said Ira, impassively, knowing that everytime her mother smiled slyly, it meant something that would irk Ira.

"Well, your friend Dimple called this morning," said Mrs Zariwala, looking askance at Ira.

"Mom! No... not Dimple..." whined Ira.

"And, she's called you over to her place today. Honey, look, I know you don't like her, but Dimple's a really polite girl, and saying 'no' to her seems really rude," said her mother, consolingly.

Dimple Mirchandani was an overly-sweet girl, according to Mrs Zariwala, but the truth was known only to Ira. Dimple was an unusually timid girl. She slumped on Ira for everything, and went with everything Ira said. Dimple's odd behaviour was incomprehensible, but nonetheless, she was polite.

An hour later, an unusually audacious horn filled the air with its jarring sound. It was Dimple's mother, sitting in her sedan, parked in the driveway of the Zariwalas. Waving goodbye to Mrs Zariwala, Ira trotted down the stairs and reached the car.

"Hello, Ira dear," said Mrs Mirchandani, airily. Mrs Mirchandani was a tall woman, with long, wavy hair. Her face was an amalgamation of rib tickling features- pig like eyes, excessively threaded, thinned down eyebrows, tiny ears, a nose like a baby corn and cheeks gleaming as a reminder of the countless facials they'd been subjected to.

"Morning aunty. How are you?" said Ira, trying her best to be nice.

"Oh, I'm good. Dimple's at home. We'll pick her up and go shopping together," said Mrs Mirchandani. Shopping. That was a terrible blow, especially when it was Dimple who was going to be her accompaniment, Ira thought.

They drove smoothly for a while, then turned into a wide lane, that led to a single, colossal villa. Brown and gritty walls, marble statues, a fountain made of crystal, so one couldn't tell the difference between the water and its source, a huge archway and and a gawdy entrance- affluence at its best.

A tall, ruddy skinned, svelte girl was standing next to an outdoor aquarium. She had eyes in the shape of perfect, tiny pearls coloured brown, black locks that went down from her head till her waist and a perfect smile adorned with dimples.

"Dimpy! Come on in," said Ira.

Dimple walked up to the car, running her fingers through her locks. Giving a warm smile, she said, "So, we're off for shopping, aren't we?"

Her mother nodded. Soon, they were out on the main road which was bustling with the noise of the city's work goers' vehicles. Mrs Mirchandani pushed a button on the music console and the radio got turned on. She seemed expectant.

The channel played its tagline and then a music jockey began speaking:

"So, good morning every one! Today, is our first show with the gorgeous, stunning, Mrs Mirchandani!" said the woman.

"Oh, Aditi, thank you for this lovely introduction, but I'm sure our listeners would want to know what my weekly show on your radio station is really about," said Mrs Mirchandani.

"Definitely. So, for all our beloved listeners, I am going to introduce Mrs Mirchandani once again. She is a renowned public speaker and has conducted several workshops on the development of interpersonal relationships. She has a vast knowledge of soft skills and is a true humanitarian.

We've brought you this show, so that Mrs Mirchandani can give you some tips on the development of your soft skills. So, stay tuned and join us every week on Monday

and Thursday, right here!" said the jockey
with great gusto.

"At ten in the morning, everyone!" added
Mrs Mirchandani.

"Yes. Time for a break now. We'll continue
with Mrs Mirchandani. Stay tuned!"

Mrs Mirchandani was smiling. Ira was stunned. This really was some great news. She hoped Dimple would pick up some tips from her mother. Mrs Mirchandani was indeed a well known speaker. Ira had attended a few seminars with her mother. They had been inspiring.

"I shall from now on be going to the studio for recording my shows. Every Saturday and Sunday. Anyway, how'd you like it, Ira?" said Mrs Mirchandani, gleefully.

"Oh, it was amazing, aunty. All the best to you," said Ira.

Soon, they turned into a parking lot. "Stop, please," said the boy in charge. Mrs Mirchandani's lips curved downwards. She pulled out some cash, paid the required amount and took the parking ticket from the boy.

Ira noticed that Mrs Mirchandani had now got a frown settled on her face. Then, Mrs Mirchandani started, "Charging twenty rupees for two hours is ridiculous! I'm pretty sure these boys slip five bucks into their pockets!"

Ira and Dimple didn't break the silence. Ira looked at Dimple who was glaring outside. She didn't seem affected at all. Her countenances were still those of calm and quiet. Dimple turned towards Ira and gave a vague smile, the kind she always gave. Ira returned a weak smile- she couldn't help thinking what made Dimple behave awkwardly.

Mrs Mirchandani parked the car and slid out. Ira and Dimple followed.

Thud.

Dimple had closed the door with too much vigour. "What's this? Can't you be soft?" said Mrs Mirchandani, looking cross.

Dimple still seemed unaffected. To Ira, it appeared as if Mrs Mirchandani's voice only fell on Dimple's ears, never flowed in to vibrate the drum. She then turned to Ira and whispered, cautious enough not to let her mother hear what she was saying, "Keep watching my mother. You'll see why I do the same".

Ira nodded apprehensively. They strode up the stairs of the parking lot and reached the main market. "So, we're going to some mall, I suppose?" said Ira.

"Oh, you want to go to a mall, is it?" said Mrs Mirchandani, confused.

"If it's not okay, we surely can go to some other place," said Ira, struggling to be polite.

They ambled down a lane, then took a left turn and walked straight, until they reached a huge market, where several stalls and shacks had been set up. Vendors were screaming at the highest frequencies they could manage, trying to garner as many buyers as possible. The streets were strewn with toffee-wrappers and polythene bags, not to mention a stinking smell issuing from a manhole somewhere nearby.

Mrs Mirchandani pointed to a shop made of bricks red as fire, cement visible in the joints of the bricks. Mrs Mirchandani paced towards the shop, the two girls trotting behind her.

"Good morning, Wasim ji. I'm here for the suit I saw last time. I hope you've thought about it," she said, narrowing her pig like eyes.

Wasim's face turned into a ball of fire. Blood gushed into his pale cheeks. On his forehead, crooked lines appeared like cracks on a drought stricken piece of earth. His lips curved downwards.

"Mom had a row with this salesman last week over this suit she wanted," whispered Dimple to Ira. She continued, "It isn't very expensive, given how good it is. Eight thousand rupees is not much for something made of pure silk and hand embroidered designs".

"I'm sorry, but no. I'm constant on the price I had told you last time," said Wasim, curtly. "Please, can nothing be done? I'm sure you do get a huge margin on these suits!" roared Mrs Mirchandani.

"If *you're* too miser to chuck out a few notes from your pocket for this excellent piece of art, then I'm afraid, I do not have time to spare for a debate that's going to have no end at all!" said Wasim and scorned.

Mrs Mirchandani looked affronted. Ira couldn't construe the reason for Mrs Mirchandani's disapproval regarding payment of any sort. She seemed to be wanting everything at a price lower than the quoted one.

"And, by the way, he's all ready come down to eight thousand from the original eleven," said Dimple to Ira. Ira let out a low whine. Her first day of summer vacations was treating her miserably.

"Fine then," said Mrs Mirchandani and took a long sniff so that her lungs got filled with air enough to support her next scream, "I am not paying you a rupee more than five thousand for this tacky, rotten piece of cloth! You all... all of you, small people! Ambitionless! Instead of accepting my patronage, you're showing me that haughty face! Never mind now. Dimple, Ira... get moving".

"*Patronage?* Patronage, did you say? We don't need patronage. We earn through pure hard work! And, we're honest in the prices we quote! Don't come back! Ever!" said Wasim, his voice fading away as Mrs Mirchandani and the girls moved away from the shop, into the main marketplace once again.

Dimple then nudged her mother and said, "The cobbler...you forgot. We've to go to him. He has dad's shoes, remember?"

Mrs Mirchandani nodded and turned right. The present lane was gloomy, but the air was fresher. A crispy aroma of fresh, new shoes was flowing through the air. Occassionally, the smell of shoe polish also went up the nostrils. They stalled their legs in front of a small shack that housed many repaired shoes, a number of instruments and shoe polishes and a lanky man who seemed like the cobbler, given the streaks of black and brown shoe polish on his hands. "Ramesh ji, I had come to you last week, remember?" said Mrs Mirchandani, trying to keep her cool.

"Of course, I remember. I've mended the shoes, but it's really taken me a lot of time, you know. So a little extra money for the extra effort put in..." he said, looking expectant.

"How much?" she said, tersely.

"A hundred and twenty five rupees," he said.

"You'd quoted seventy five rupees, I recall," she said.

"But I just said..."

"No, you did not. Hundred rupees at the maximum, that's it!" she screeched.

"Okay, okay," he submitted.

"Filthy scoundrel," Mrs Mirchandani muttered under her breath as pulled out a note from her purse.

"Miserly woman. The whole city knows how rich she is. Doesn't have the courtsey to pay the poor their due," he too muttered.

Taking the money from Mrs Mirchandani, he said, "You know, this is the third time you've got these shoes repaired..." And saying so, he smirked.

Mrs Mirchandani glared at him with a frown. Ira broke the silence. "So, where to next? Ice cream, anyone?" Dimple giggled and said, "Yes, sure. That's a nice way to *beat the heat*". Ira still couldn't see why anyone should deny a fair share of money to someone who deserved it, especially when it came to the super rich, Mrs Mirchandani.

Mrs Mirchandani-the saintly public speaker-seemed to be at a loss of her own skills-the soft skills.

The trio sped past the cobbler's. Mrs Mirchandani seemed cross. Soon, they got to an ice cream vendor. Without asking for preferences, Mrs Mirchandani bought two of the cheapest ice creams available. She paid and the trio sped to the parking lot.

"Hello Mrs Khandelwal! I hope everything's good," Mrs Mirchandani said, mildly smiling. Mrs Khandelwal was a neighbour of the Mirchandanis. She was the sort of woman who would smile broadly at someone, while meticulously observing the person's behaviour to gossip about it later. "Oh yes, Mira, everything's fine," said Mrs Khandelwal. Just then, a man, dressed in a tattered shirt and pants came and put forth a bowl. He jingled the coins in the bowl and looked expectantly at Mrs Mirchandani.

Mrs Mirchandani rummaged inside her purse. Mrs Khandelwal's eyes peered into Mrs Mirchandani's purse, as much as they could. Mrs Mirchandani looked askance at Mrs Khandelwal and noticed Mrs Khandelwal's large, greenish blue eyes scanning her purse intently.

Mrs Mirchandani pulled out a note of a hundred rupees and put it in his bowl. The beggar thanked her and happily left. "You know, Mrs Khandelwal, I totally love helping the poor! I feel blessed, really," she said, putting her chin up. "Of course, I know. You're indeed so nice," said Mrs Khandelwal, gave a broad smile and strolled past them.

Ira felt strange. The woman, who haggled with all her might should've been all the more miserly when things came to charity, she thought. She nudged Dimple. "What was that?" said Ira.

"Soft skills, you know. Mom delivers lectures on how to behave nicely with people, be them rich or poor. But those are lectures...sermons...they're meant to be delivered to *other people's* ears, not her own," said Dimple, looking scathingly at her mother.

"What do you mean?" said Ira, dumbfounded.

"She never tells the other side...which says: *Behave according to who's standing next to you.* That's what she did just now, when Mrs Khandelwal was here".

"But...but, your mum...she's an expert on communication skills, ethics, soft skills..." said Ira.

Dimple chuckled. "Yes, that's what she tells everyone. I mean, she's a certified expert on these social skills, but preachers are seldom practitioners," said Dimple, looking at infinity.

A few days later, a scorching hot Monday morning greeted the residents of the Zariwala villa. There had been an electricity cut since five in the morning in the locality where the Zariwalas lived. And now, the thermometer had become high on mercury.

"Mom, how about we go to a mall?" said Ira.

"A mall? For what?"

"There are air conditioners in a mall... and we do need a break from this dratted mass of bricks radiating heat," she said.

"That's a good idea, then," said Mrs Zariwala.

In a matter of minutes, the duo got ready, locked the house and hopped into their sedan. As they drove out of the locality, Mrs Zariwala said, "Now that we're out, let's turn some music on, should we?"

Ira nodded and turned the radio on:

> *"Hello and welcome back! Here's Mrs Mirchandani and she's got some really nice advice for us today," said the radio jockey with great gusto.*
>
> *"Oh yes, yes, I do. What I'm going to tell today is an essential part of a wise man's personality. Last week, I went to the market with my daughter and her friend. I had to*

buy a suit. Initially, when the shopkeeper quoted the price, I found it a little too much. But then, I kept my thoughts to myself and quietly paid the price asked for, because I realized that a lot of hard work had gone into the making of that suit. And I respect that hard work. Besides, not everyone's rich, and the poor deserve their due!" said Mrs Mirchandani.

"What a beautiful–"

Ira switched the channel.

"Why did you switch the channel?" asked Mrs Zariwala.

"Because her story's only as true as somebody telling you that the Sun rises in the West," said Ira, looking thoughtfully out of the window.

6

THE WORST PART OF LOVE

It was a Thursday. "Ma! Ma! I'm back from school," said Rimjhim, as she scooted towards her mother-Antara's room.

"Yes, darling, I know. Now, quickly go and change. And, then we'll have lunch together.

Thursdays were special for Rimjhim. A Thursday was the only day in a week that she found her mother at home, after getting back from school. Antara was a busy woman. She had suffered 15 years of raising her daughter, Rimjhim, which had been a tedious job; not because her husband didn't help her but ….her husband couldn't help her.

Anurag, her husband, was dead. That was the conundrum. Antara was a dermatologist by profession. She worked from 9am to 7pm every day, except Thursdays, which were half days. Sundays were for tutoring 3 children from her locality.

Antara gave Rimjhim a burger. Rimjhim sank into the burger. The gooey cheese, mayonnaise oozed out and attempted to reach her wrists on the way to the elbows but nay her tongue would direct every drop of it into the mouth. The burger was delicious, for it had been made by none other than Antara.

"Ma, there's phomphing that I'fe been wanting to f.. tell you" said Rimjhim, her mouth stuffed with the burger she was gorging on.

Next "Yes dear, tell me, what is it?" said Antara gliding a glass of water across the table. "It is about this guy I really like. He is in my class and well, well! He has the most mesmerizing face of all times!" said Rimjhim turning pink.

"Aha ha! Is that all? You are so sweet Rimjhim," said Antara. "Uh..Ma, why don't you tell me something about your crushes as a child? I really want to know," said Rimjhim and made a puppy face.

Antara was delighted with Rimjhim's request. She thought, perhaps, she would get to spend some quality time with her daughter. In addition, she had always wanted to narrate her love story to her daughter. This opportunity seemed fertile enough to plant her story in Rimjhim's memory.

"My story, eh? Well, umm… okay," said Antara. "Yay! Finally! I thought I wouldn't be able to persuade you," said Rimjhim, her eyes twinkling with joy. "Ok, Ok, so it goes on something like this: I was 15 years old and was in 10th grade. There was this guy, a year senior. I didn't know this guy so well. We had spoken once earlier. I had seen him in school, sometimes. And that was all I knew about him. Just another acquaintance." Antara's cheeks changed colors within many hues of red. Rimjhim had not seen her Mom in this phase of emotion earlier and was surprised and well as amused. Antara took notice of the expressions on Rimjhim's face and became distracted and slightly irritated. "Did I say that I am done with my story?" asked Antara. "No, no, continue please, I am all ears" said the eager daughter. "Fine, so listen and no more interruptions please" said Antara with a firm but affectionate voice. "He was a normal looking guy: tall, lanky, with a peach complexion. He was good at academics, so I had heard. Since we had hardly communicated I never cared to know about him. 17th February, the Sunday, I was basking in the early morning Sun in my lawn, preparing for the final exams which were due shortly. It was an otherwise routine boring day. The same mundane routine. The fruitwala was making the morning round. The newspaper tossed over the gate. The community dog lazing around with legs up in the air. Some old men and women in grey and blue attire were jogging and few young people in whites and greens, cycling. And then it happened! The same guy slowly jogged passed our gate. He cast a glance in and at the same moment I happened to see him. Our eyes met. It seemed a routine affair. Many times guys would peep into homes of young girls.

Monday came. It was the same. Studies, dog, newspaper, jogging, cycling, Sun, more studies and exams were one day nearer. He passed again. Same thing happened again. I was a bit cross but forgot quickly as I immersed back into my book. Tuesday, nothing happened. Wednesday too, it was the same mundane routine. Was I missing him? Yes, to my surprise! I was waiting to see it happen again. Thursday came. Thereafter seeing him was a daily event. He always cast a look inside through the gate." Antara's face blossomed with hues of pink. Rimjhim asked "Did you talk to him? Ever approached him, Ma?"

"Oh no! I didn't. He did, though. But honestly it was by far the silliest meeting I have ever had," said Antara, her eyebrows tightening. She pursed her lips and began striking the table with her fingers. Then with a nod of disapproval, she said, "Well that meeting ….it happened a month after I saw him jogging past our house. But before that too, there were some instances that sufficed for … umm…if not solid conclusions then at least conjectures.

The first clue came on a day when he had been jogging past my house everyday for more than a week. That day he stopped in front of the gate of my house to check the time on his watch. I'm pretty sure that it was a well chalked out plan to begin a conversation with me. We looked at each other and he smiled. Oh yes, he smiled," said Antara, blushing.

"Incredible! Then did you both wave at each other?" said Rimjhim, indeed alacritous to listen.

"Yes, a few days later, he did wave at me. That first wave set my heart pounding furiously enough to break my ribs, I'd say. When waving lost its charm, I decided to approach him and start talking to him. So one day, I stood outside the gate. But I saw no movement anywhere. Nothing, not even a leaf rustled.

And to my utter disappointment, he didn't turn up that day," she said.

Rimjhim looked at her mother with great intent. She had never seen her mother going through so many swings of mood in just one conversation. She had always known her mother as a serious, determined woman who didn't speak much. She hadn't even anticipated that her mother would've had any serious crushes as a child.

Antara had always veiled her true self from her daughter. The miserable times she'd gone through had incapacitated her ability to laugh, or worse, to smile. The veil had been now lifted because of a wind called Rimjhim. Antara had started by looking askance at her love story, shy to narrate it. But now, what she wanted most was to delve into the sea of her memories and pull out from its depths, all the parts of her love story.

Antara continued, "For many days then, he was nowhere to be seen. But, one day, all the cards flipped into my favor. I remember, I was sitting in the lawn, trying hard to solve a numerical in Physics. I was truly scratching my head, turning my beautiful locks into a haystack!

Then someone patted my shoulder. I turned my head around and it was the same, average looking, lanky guy. He offered to help. Without any delay I handed him pen and paper and he solved it so fluently that I began doubting if he had composed the question and not the book's author. I looked at him in bewilderment. Then I said something which I guess I shouldn't have".

Rimjhim raised her right eyebrow. She could make out a slight regret in her mother's eyes. "What did you say?"

"I said that he was the most handsome guy I'd ever set eyes on. And I still remember his countenance turning into those of surprise. With shaking hands he put the pen and paper down onto the table and hurried out of the gate," said Antara. She regretted her deed a lot. That sentence was truly a misfit for the commencement of any conversation.

Rimjhim couldn't believe her mother's confession. Then straightening herself up, she said, "How did this average looking guy turn to handsome, all of a sudden?"

"Oh, well… I'd started liking him, so naturally, my perceptions about him changed. You'll discover this as you grow. All of a sudden, my eyes showed me a more adorable, a more likeable guy."

"Let us now resume the story. He turned up the next day and I apologized. He chuckled and gave a broad grin. Then, he raised his hand, brought it close to my forehead and tucked my hair behind my ear and said, 'You too, are beautiful, very beautiful'. I froze for a minute- he had caressed me. I wondered if it meant love, then asked my mind to deny such allegations and asked it to come back to the present where he was still standing before me. Unable to think of anything else, I asked him where he'd been all the past days he'd not jogged. He told me he'd gone to his grandparents' place in Kanpur. Then he asked my name and said 'This seems like a nice start...uh... Antara, that's the name, right? A beautiful one, I must say'. I do not remember anyone else to have showered such compliments in a row, except him," said Antara, lifting her fringes to wipe the sweat off her forehead.

Rimjhim gazed at her mother in astonishment. She wished to keep listening to this story forever. Then Antara resumed, "Soon, we became great friends. He helped me with my studies, instead of jogging. He narrated some incidents when he'd seen me in school, one of which was quarrelling with the man at the canteen. I felt abashed at first, but then he told me that he admired me for it. When I asked him why, he responded, 'This shows you're vigorous enough to deal with people. Most people aren't, you know'. I simply couldn't believe his perspicacity! I'd never thought of this habit the other way round".

Rimjhim too couldn't believe his niceness. She'd so far come across boys who were only good enough to think about themselves and no one else.

"My parents were happy I'd found a tutor for free! But, one day when I was standing at the gate, waiting for him, my eyes met a disappointing spectacle. In the distance, I saw him accompanied by another girl, both ambling towards my house. I couldn't believe the sight. Some other girl was next to him? My mind started shooting all sorts of abuses at my heart, for my heart had poured out too much love for him, compelling my mind to think of him all the time. And now, he was with another girl. I was indeed shocked. I thought he was coming to my place so that I would meet his girlfriend. My blood began boiling. It deluged into my face, turning it red. What if he came and put in my hand his wedding invitation, I thought. But when he reached my place, he said to the other girl, 'Aarzoo, look, this is the girl. She's Antara, the girl I love. I'm sorry, but you're still a great friend of mine'. He then turned to me, looked into my eyes, and said, 'Yes Antara, I love you. You are my truth. You are…my Antara.' I was awestruck," said Antara, her eyes welling up with tears. She had recalled every incident with all its intricacies. Rimjhim hugged Antara tight.

Rimjhim was wonderstruck. She thought of her mother as an extraordinarily fortunate woman. "So, this friendship finally took another turn, right? And what about Aarzoo?" she said.

"Oh, yes. We were one, at last. My face was suffused with glee. And ah, yes, about Aarzoo. To tell you the truth, Rimjhim, I salute that woman. She said she was happy to see that the man she loved was happy. Sobbing, she quietly left.

Then of course, we began meeting more. We would sit in my garden for about two hours every day. I read more and talked less, but I feel it was his presence that was enough to make the difference. The feeling of him being near me sufficed for our dearth of conversation. He would often look at my hands, as if wanting to hold them, and never leave. I too returned a gesture of love by fondling his ears, once in a while. And, here comes the interesting part.

He used to often write small messages of love on 'Post it'. He would then stick them at the back of my text books. And for each message he stuck, I gave him a chocolate, made by me. Then, I appeared for my exams. Whatever he had taught me, came in handy, especially in Mathematics. He had a knack for Mathematics, I feel," Antara said, gulping down some water to rehydrate her throat, which was tired of moving its vocal cords so much.

Rimjhim was now sleepy. It had been three hours since her mother had been narrating her story. But, she couldn't cease the desire to listen to this story. Then Antara said, "Rimjhim, do you know what the worst part of love is?" Rimjhim, unable to think up an answer, simply nodded sideways and said, "No, tell me about it, Ma". "It was he who told me about it. The first time he said it…well okay, I guess I have to tell you now.

It was a beautiful evening. He came to my house and without saying a word, walked straight to the door of the house, and said something to my mother. My mother squeaked with joy. It turned out he was an old family friend's son and his father had called us over for dinner that night. I couldn't believe how supportive fortune could become. So, I got ready hurriedly, because I didn't want to be late at *his* party! I dressed up in a new midi I had bought off late and wore one of my best stilettos. Then, I drew a fine line of eyeliner on my eyelids, careful to avoid the lashes. At last, I applied a layer of lip gloss and drew a comb down my hair, making sure they looked wavy. We reached the party and soon excused ourselves from the drawing room crowd. Then, he took me for a stroll in his garden, much bigger than mine! We ambled slowly across the garden and settled down on a bench. Then, he asked me, 'Antara, do you know what the worst part of love is?' 'No, you tell me', I said. He clutched my hand tightly and looked up at the star studded sky. He then turned towards me, put an arm around my back and tugged me closer to him. He then smoothly lifted my fringes, tucked them behind my left ear. Gazing into my eyes, he said, 'The worst part of love is that you get so engrossed in love, remember the person, gaze into the void...at infinity...and keep smiling like an idiot'. I chuckled and replied, 'I guess we are the biggest idiots then!' That party was awesome," said Antara, smiling like an idiot!

"Oh my! What happened after that? Tell me quick, tell me!" said Rimjhim, all ears. Antara didn't look as mirthful now. Her smile had curved slightly downward.

Yet, she continued, "After this lovely conversation, we became all the more comfortable around each other. At his birthday party, we danced like professionals! Credits to me, since I danced and still dance well! But then... one day... it was the twenty fifth of June, when school resumed and I didn't spot him there. I hadn't met him or talked to him for some days. I thought he was cross and so hadn't come to school. But when I got home, I found a letter. I do not know how he managed to deliver it, though. I'll tell you what it read:

> *'Antara, please, please don't look for me. All of a sudden we've had to move out of the city. Dad has lost his job and so we've migrated to a suburb. Do not ask where, please. It's a serious family matter and frankly, I do not know much about it. All I know is that he's lost a job–I guess because of the ongoing recession–that he'd worked really hard to get. I will meet you, if fate makes us meet dear.*

> *Bye*
> *Love you and always will'.*

I was shocked. I searched desperately, called him, e-mailed him, texted him, but to no avail.

"So, he betrayed you?" asked Rimjhim, in consternation.

Antara seemed lost. She had become drenched in love. Rimjhim nudged her and Antara took a deep breath. Finally, she resumed, "Huh? No... Anyway...for the next five years, he didn't show up anywhere but in my dreams. I would see him and rush to him. He would extend his arm, his beautiful hand longing to clasp mine. But, before I could get to him, he would fade away...Oh, those nightmares..."

"Funny thing is, I had such dreams for the five years when I was attending college. Then, one night came, when he didn't come in my dream. Next morning, I woke up, the freshest in five years. It was also the day of the last exam of the last year in college. I went out onto the balcony of the hostel and gazed up at the sky. It was well, twilight, then. A long trail of shimmering lights passed across the sky. It was an airplane, but something about it struck me. I too had my flight that evening. I got dressed, did a bit of last minute revision and went straight to the examination hall. At the entrance, a quote had been engraved by some student which said: Love is Endurance. I couldn't help, but smile. At seven in the evening, I was sitting at the airport, sipping coffee. Then..."

Antara giggled. Her cheeks reddened. "Then, a heavy, silky smooth voice said, 'May I sit here?' I looked up. The tall guy, handsome guy, was standing right there. I got up instantly. He held his hand out and I clasped it...

clasped it with so much vigor; I feared I might've caused the veins in his hand to rupture. But, I was not going to let go. Not this time. He hugged me and closed his arms tightly around my back. I could hear our hearts beating and throbbing hard. He lifted my fringes, and smiled.

We were both flying to Delhi. Both of us had our ancestral homes there, you know. We met often...we were a happy couple. For three years, we were perhaps the most joyous pair of humans. For three years...until..."

Antara paused. She became morose and tiny pearls of perspiration accumulated on her upper lip and her palms.

Rimjhim, unable to guess, said "Until, he shifted again, I assume?"

"Yes...shifted...shifted away, forever..." said Antara, her eyes reddening.

"What was his problem, Ma? What made him so unstable? You really should've asked," whined Rimjhim.

"His problem...I don't know...why, why did it happen?" said Antara, sobbing.

"Don't tell me, he actually broke up? I mean, he left you?" said Rimjhim, exasperated.

"No, no... He didn't leave me...he...*he left everyone*. Oh...he was coming to see me. Rimjhim dear, I had been hospitalized, and he was coming to see me. I was in Lucknow, and he... he was on a flight to Lucknow. And... And the plane...it crashed, Rimjhim. It *crashed*! Down and down he went..."

Tears were rolling down Antara's cheeks. She was looking into the void.

"Ma...I'm so sorry. First he left you and then, my dratted father. Father had betrayed you right? said Rimjhim.

Antara had always told Rimjhim that her husband had betrayed her. But there was something that kept Rimjhim confused. Whenever Antara said that her husband betrayed her, she had a slight smile on her face. Rimjhim couldn't construe the reason behind Antara's smile accompanying the utterance of such a bitter truth.

"Yes, your father betrayed me." said Antara, her lips curling upwards slightly.

"And he died too. Serves him right. Such people deserve death," said Rimjhim.

"Ma... you've told me your love story. Won't you tell me his name? It's weird that you still haven't mentioned his name even once," said Rimjhim, looking up expectantly.

"His name was... Anuraag. Anuraag Singhal," said Antara, gazing at infinity.

"Da... dad? It was dad all along? *Oh my god*! Then, why do you always say that he betrayed you? He was such a nice man!"

"Betrayed me, Anuraag did. He ditched me, because he left me alone to raise such a beautiful daughter! He ditched me because he had promised me that he will be the first one to take a photograph with you, Rimjhim!

That year we reunited, we got married. Our parents were really happy for us, I still remember. And the night I was hospitalized, I had gone into labor. But... I lost him..." said Antara, her face fraught with sadness.

Rimjhim now knew that her dad was truly amazing. *A gentleman in all ways, a true lover.*

"Ma...I now know what the worst part of love is," she said, nudging Antara softly. Antara smiled and closed her eyes for a moment to reminisce Anuraag.

She put off the lamp on her bedside. Covering herself and Rimjhim with a blanket, she closed her eyes, and sighed heavily.

The clock struck and Antara shuddered. She was happy.

~Dear Anuraag, now our daughter too knows what the worst part of love ~ Antara thought to herself.

She wanted to see Anuraag in her dream that night. She really did.

7

KNOCK, KNOCK... HYENA!

"Aha!" laughed Tori, as she packed her bag. "What are you laughing at?" Pearl asked, as she tossed a hot dog loaded with extra cheese. "Nothing, I'm just so excited...!" Tori replied, as if she were the happiest girl on Earth. "Don't laugh too much; the lions will eat you up soon, Tori!" Zayne commented, rather sardonically.

Soon, the others: Zara, Taylor and Carlos came into the room. All six of them were going on a trip to Uganda, East Africa. Each one was nearly done with his or her packing. They had assembled at Tori's place to meet up one last time before the trip. After discussing the last moment points, they bade goodbye to Tori and went back to their homes.

The next day was fun filled. Everyone was quacking in their boots. They boarded the flight and soon, they were off from Canada to Uganda.

The airplane was a true treat for everyone aboard. The cabin was spacious, the seats were wide and the food trays were loaded with fruits, turkey, chicken rolls, cheese and pepper sausages, lettuce and spinach sandwiches topped with mayonnaise, walnut and chocolate muffins, lemonade and bottled water.

In about ten and a half hours, they were in Kampala. Everyone aboard got off the aircraft. A taxi took the six friends to their hotel. "Here you are," said Mr. Charles Kabumba. "Please, I hope you'll turn up, whenever we'll need you," Zayne said as he paid the money. "Definitely, I will. You can call me Charles," he said replied smilingly in his African accent. Mr. Charles would be their guide and friend for the rest of their lives. They didn't know this.

Next day after breakfast, they took a tourist bus from Kampala to Queen Elizabeth National Park. The drive was mesmerizing. They passed through the savannah, gentle slopes westwards towards the Great Rift Valley and the quiet villages with busy people working in the fields. By late afternoon they had reached the main gate of the national park by the highway where they got down and took a closed Land Rover taxi for the ride into the national park. They were booked into the best of the national park resorts on this side of the Atlantic: Mweya Safari lodge. As they entered the national park, it was quiet; very very quiet. The vehicle was moving slowly. Suddenly it stopped. A herd of wild elephants about 9 in number were crossing the road with a calf moving blight fully between the legs of the Mummy elephant.

Wild elephants crossing with the bubbly calf

The Land Rover moved on. There were few antelopes returning home. A dead carcass of a wild boar was lying besides the track. It was left behind by a satisfied carnivore. They entered the Mweya Safari lodge gates. Wow! The neatly manicured garden with statues of animals in the pathway, were a sight to behold. The luxurious lobby of the hotel had already spelt the comforts of the rooms. Each had a separate room booked. Everyone except Tori, slept off. Tori, had always been very inquisitive. She went downstairs to the reception. "Miss, I'm hungry. Where's the restaurant again?" she asked. "Over there, to the right." "Thank you".

Tori went to the restaurant. The place was carved out of wood. The roof was sloping and rested on standing,

Antelopes crossing

long logs of wood. Artful, local handicraft chandeliers were hanging from it. Sunlight peered through the small windows that had ornate African designs. The aroma of fresh coffee beans complimented the serene surrounding. There were three walls made only of wood while the fourth one had a huge glass fixed in it. Tori walked to the glass window and stood there, gazing at the deer outside. "Beautiful, aren't they?" someone said to Tori. Tori looked to her side. It was the manager. "Yes, indeed they are. May I go and meet them, like face to face?" Tori asked. "Yes you may, miss. But, remember, we are responsible for your protection, only till the time you are within the cemented boundaries of the resort building, leave alone the grass of the lawn also. The moment you step down from the resorts' stairs, you are in the territory of the animals here. Remember, we are an invading force in their territory. *We* have built *our* home, in *their* home.

Flamingoes!

The animals are at transitory peace with us. If we will break the treaty, they will retaliate too". A shiver ran down Tori's spine. "Yes mister, you are right". Then, someone shouted from behind. "Madam! Your food is ready. Please have it". Tori paced towards her table. The waiter said, "Do have your food and let me know you liked it. Enjoy". Tori had some of the local delicacies. They were indeed enjoyable. "Yummy, that was a sumptuous meal. I loved it!" Tori said, overjoyed.

Soon, the others walked down to the restaurant. After having their fill, they decided to devote their time to a game of scrabble. The next day, everyone was ready with their back packs. Mr. Charles arrived at half past four in the morning, with their driver James Oryem Makubuyaand,

James in short. They jumped into the huge Land Rover and made their way through the national park. Queen Elizabeth national park in Western Uganda is a huge area by all standards. It is impossible to see the entire park even in one week time also. It is large, almost two thousand square kilometer swathe of territory.

The sky was pitch dark. Their first meeting was with a hippo that just raised his head from his morning breakfast of grass grazing. It was just five meters from the road bending. The headlights were on as the sun had still not broken out of the darkness. The hippo's eyes were gleaming green. The car swerved to right on the bend and the hippo got back to business: grazing. James told the tourists that hippos are good lawn mowers. Charles wondered aloud if he should keep one as a pet to mow the lawn in his house, which was strewn with grass as high as the hedge. That would at least make his wife happy! They all laughed.

As time passed, the sky started changing colours. At first, it turned purple with traces of scarlet. Then, as it seemed to human eyes, the colours blended smoothly, like paint. The clouds seemed like soft and fluffy, beautifully coloured cotton balls. The sky became pinkish blue. The sun's rays peered through minute holes in the clouds. Then slowly, the clouds lit up at the borders. Gradually, the clouds drifted apart and the sun came into view, shining with its tremendous glory. And then just in a

Salt lake

while, it was a bright morning. The Land rover moved on. And then it stopped. At least a hundred antelopes were crossing the dirt track where they were driving.

As the day broke out they saw wild boars, elephants, wild buffaloes, black and white colobus monkeys, eagles and more. "Oh, look! Flamingoes by the water body! Quick, someone snap a picture," Tori said. Zayne took his camera out and clicked a few snaps. The sight was indeed mesmerizing. Nobody had ever seen the world so closely. Yes, the world. What world would it be if there were no animals, no plants? No thick foliage, no flora, no fauna? What if there would be grey concrete buildings and black roads everywhere? So boring it would have

The leopard was resting on its right paw
and moving its tail slowly

been. They passed by some dried salt lakes, which James said was frequented by animals for salt licking. Nature was amazing indeed.

The vehicle came to a halt. In an excited tone, James said, "Now everyone. Look to your right. There won't be anything more enchanting than what you'll see now. Just don't open the windows". Everyone turned to where James was pointing. "What?" asked Pearl. "Be quiet. I can feel the presence of a leopard. Look there up on the tree. I can see it sitting on a branch, not far away. Look it is resting its head on its right paw and is moving his tail slowly." Others saw nothing for a long time that seemed hours. They moved on in silence thinking that James had played a trick on them.

Afternoon was spent aboard the double decker boat on the Kasinga Channel which connects Lake Edward and Lake George, a part of the Great Rift Valley lakes and host to large number of crocodiles, hippos, eagles and elephants on the islands in between. Of course there were flamingoes along with a number of different varieties of other birds.

By evening eight o'clock they were dead tired and were reflecting on the satisfying day they had. While the others retired to the rooms after a quick bite, Tori, Carlos and Taylor were just lazing around at the table, munching on some garlic bread and orange juice, reflecting on the day's events. Tori looked at Carlos, with a feeling of regret. Both said it almost together, "We didn't see any carnivore cats! No lions, no cheetahs, no leopards." They were told by the waiter Amey Kakooza, that lion sighting was pretty common and was last seen a day before, just beside the garden restaurant at Mweya Safari lodge about fifty meters from where they were dining now. The tourist lodge was located right in middle of the national park, so it was no surprise.

Just then two Indians who were sitting on the next table waved at Carlos and joined their table. "Hi, I am Sher Shah and this is my wife Haydara." Carlos, Tori and Taylor greeted them. "What all did you see?" Tori narrated all the day's events and the animals they had seen. "Any lions or leopards?" asked Sher Shah. "Nope, except you" said Carlos with a disappointed voice but

Hippos and wild buffaloes at the Kasinga channel

with a smile. Carlos had studied some Arabic as part of a school exchange programme. Sher meant lion and Haydara meant lioness in Arabic. Sher Shah and Haydara caught on and laughed heartily. "We saw tree climbing lions last year at Ishasha Park, the southern part of this national park, but none in this sector during this visit," said Haydara. "Tree climbing lions! But we had learnt that lions cannot climb trees!" exclaimed Tori. "You see them only here at Ishasha" said Sher Shah. "But we saw hyenas, that too huge ones, today" whispered Sher Shah. "But hyenas are not very common in this park, "said Taylor. "Yes, true. They are in this sector today, just a kilometer from this lodge. We saw them about an hour ago. On the air strip behind the lodge" said Haydara. Meanwhile Sher

Shah's mobile got buzzing and he alongwith Haydara excused themselves and went towards their rooms.

Charles and James happened to pass by. Tori said, "Please, give me your Land Rover, James. I promise, I'll keep it safe. I want to go on one last ride. As such, tomorrow, we all shall be leaving for Mozambique. So please, let me go…" She didn't finish. James was shocked and surprised. He said "No". He was firm. Charles too nodded his head in disapprovingly. "It is too dangerous. And it is night time too. Not permitted in the national park. I have the license. You don't. Sorry please." Saying this they sat down on a nearby table for a glass of beer. The Land Rover keys along with Charles' mobile and a small bag were kept on the empty table next to where Charles and James were sitting.

Tori was not satisfied with the answer. Carlos, Tori and Taylor kept sitting for about ten minutes. Suddenly Charles and James were found to be away from the table. Charles was on the mobile and James possibly had gone to the restroom. The Land Rover keys were invitingly looking towards Tori and within a flash of a moment Tori snapped them in her pocket and rushed out. Carlos and Taylor were too surprised, and just followed suit. Tori fervently hopped in to the Land Rover and asked if anyone wished to come along. Before they realized, Taylor and Carlos hopped in though reluctantly. Arguing with Tori never won anybody anything. In a matter of few seconds, the Land Rover was out of the hotel complex towards the airstrip. The airstrip appeared to be rarely used although it was in a state of good repair. It was a pretty short one, for the types of a six to eight seater plane to land.

As they drove, they saw the most beautiful moonrise of their lives. "This moonrise is... beautiful! What do you say?" Tori asked Carlos. "I don't *think*... I know and I feel that it is beautiful. Beautiful as you are...," Carlos said as he stared at the sky. There was silence. Tori was dumbstruck. She had no reply. Taylor too kept quiet. After a while, they reached almost the middle stretch of the airstrip. The bush was dense on both sides. They had crossed few wild buffaloes on the left and a hippo on the right, mowing as usual. A few hundred meters further, Carlos exclaimed "Stop and look on the right! A Hyena!" Tori stopped. They all looked. Time froze for few seconds. Slowly they turned right, ninety degrees and were now directly facing the hyena. Without stopping the motion they continued the U turn and started driving back in the direction they had come from. About three hundred meters on, Taylor said "Tori, can we turn back and have a look at the hyenas again?" Tori was all game, as usual. She promptly turned back even before Carlos could say anything. Carlos was dumbstruck. They were turning back to see the hyena again! What if the vehicle broke down in the middle of the night? Anyway, that was past. They were near the hyena again. Again a slow U turn, face the hyena, this time two of them and then back on the return journey. All were excited, sweating, adrenaline rushing and hearts pounding. This time it was Carlos. "Tori, once more!" "What? Again? Are you mad? *Et tu* Carlos?" Tori exclaimed. But she didn't wait for an answer. Before Carlos or Taylor could say "Jack Robinson" the Land Rover was again cruising towards the direction of the hyenas. They reached same spot. Turned right ninety degrees on the runway and were facing the hyenas. Then it happened. The Land Rover coughed and choked and choked. The engine rumbling became slower and muffled and finally mute. Tori said "Cool! No problem! I must have left the accelerator". She turned the key. Few unsuccessful respiratory efforts later by the engine, it was pronounced dead. Stone dead it was.

The Land Rover with Tori, Carlos and Taylor was standing perpendicular to the airstrip, in the middle of it. Two hyenas were mocking them at thirty meters slightly off to the directions of both the headlights. All silence. Dark night with the moon rising in the distant hills and the thick savannah bush was witness to the horror. The time was around nine at night. Here were two hyenas, three friends and an engine dead vehicle in the middle of a national park in East Africa, teaming with wildlife. What an adventure! The same thought was racing through the minds of all friends. How comfortable they were few minutes ago munching a dinner of garlic bread and orange juice. And suddenly here they were, ready as dinner for the hyenas. "Switch off the headlights," Carlos mumbled. Tori did exactly as told.

Taylor was anxious, his face was flushed and he was extremely vexed. The hyena was giving spiteful looks. Suddenly, it got up from where it was sitting and paced towards the Land Rover. It sniffed all the tyres, the bonnet and the spoilers. Having done all of this, it walked and sat at a distance of about two meters from the Land Rover. Then, it howled with head up in the sky as if inviting his clan for a sumptuous meal. There were replies, many replies. A series of howls began. "Look straight" Carlos' face turned pale. Two more hyenas appeared. They sat at a further distance of about 20 meters from the vehicle ahead.

There was silence. Time had come to a standstill. Tori's throat choked. She felt sharp canines dig into her neck. It was painful. Her breathing was getting tighter. The hyena was stinking. The fur was choking her. Her t shirt was wet with her blood. Her vision was failing. Carlos whispered and shook her. "We have to do something!" Tori recovered from the short dream."I know, but who shall explain the situation to this overly adventurous girl sitting next to me? I'm sure Tori that you want to go outside and do salsa with these hyenas! After all, that would be adventure, huh?" Taylor said in the most disgusted tone. "Okay! Take it easy. Now, do as I tell you to," Tori said. "What?!" Carlos and Taylor exclaimed together. Peeping outside the window, Tori said, "Taylor, give me your cell phone. Or better, just call up Charles". Taylor attempted as told. There was no network.

Then, one hyena got up from its place, came closer to the Land Rover and sat there. This happened unnoticed. Suddenly, there was a loud bang on the rear right door of the vehicle. The door had got dented from outside and had been pushed inside. Taylor screamed loudly and burst into tears. A hyena had tried to break the car open. The other hyenas outside were hooting and growling loudly. Then they moved back. Another hyena rushed towards the bonnet of the car and banged into it. It hurt itself but the bonnet got severely damaged. The three inside the Land Rover were crying desperately for help, but in vain. "Tori, why? What was the urgency of coming here?" Carlos said, in tears. Tori didn't reply. Suddenly, a hyena banged on the window next to Taylor. The window cracked.

After a while, the violent attacks stopped. The hyenas, unable to break through the car, went away about 50 meters in front of the vehicle and sat down. Now there was a reasonable distance between the vehicle and the beasts.

There was a dearth of time and a never ending turn of events. There was less hope and more desire for death, for there were no means of escape. Carlos, Tori and Taylor crouched below. Time had flown and it was half past three in the morning. Repeated attempts to call up failed.

No signal. The cell phone battery was also weakening. Suddenly two bars of signal appeared in the mobile phone screen. Taylor called up. Charles picked the phone up. "Yes, Mr. Taylor, are you…are you alright?" he said. "No, we need help! Please do something!" he replied hesitantly. Tori snatched the phone. "Sir, please help us. Please! We are in the middle of the airstrip and the Land Rover won't start. We surrounded by hyenas" she said. "I had warned you, Miss Tori. Now, you have to find a method of survival. I am sorry, but I can be of no help to you. You are stranded because that is in your fate. Or perhaps, because of your actions. I'm sorry," Charles replied bluntly. Tori, disgusted even more, disconnected the call. Charles called back. She didn't pick up. She called up James "Hello? Yeah who's this?" James said in a half drunken state. Tori said, "Hea---Hello? James, this is Tori. We're stuck. Some hyenas have surrounded us. Please come here, immediately". "Okay, okay. Charles is with me. He just told me. We are coming," he replied.

The hyenas were still waiting patiently. A thought crossed Tori's mind. Even if help came by, how will they change over from this vehicle to the other one? Carlos suggested that he and Taylor get down from the right side. Keep the right doors open as a physical shield between the beasts and them. They will push the vehicle rearwards and meanwhile Tori on the wheel will turn steering to bring it facing in the homeward direction. This way in the final position the vehicle will come in as full obstruction between the hyenas and Taylor Carlos combine. This way when help comes both vehicles can be placed parallel close by and they can quickly shift and speed away in the other vehicle.

Taylor and Carlos stepped out of the Land Rover from the right. As decided the team started maneuvering the vehicle. The vehicle came to be positioned back in homeward direction and the hyenas were on the left and Carlos and Taylor on right of the vehicle. The hyenas made no movement. A pair of lights of a Toyota SUV with Charles and James aboard could be seen in the distance speeding towards them. Seeing no sign of danger since the hyenas were now a little away and help on the way, Carlos screamed with joy, "We---we're safe!" Suddenly, a hyena growled from behind. He froze. They had not boarded the vehicle again. It was a fatal mistake. Trembling, he turned behind. The hyena was standing cheek by jowl. Carlos glared into the hyena's unkind eyes. Within a fraction of a second, the hyena turned violent and leaped onto him.

It stood on top of Carlos and snarled, as if to call the other hyenas. Carlos started struggling with the hyena. It bit off a piece of flesh on the arm and broke his right hand in doing so. "You sick, disgusting, dog! Come fight me if you can!" Tori shouted. She thrashed the hyena's back with a rope. The hyena turned to her and almost leapt onto her, when the brutally injured Carlos came in its way and pushed Tori aside. Once again, the hyena jumped onto Carlos and gave him an injury. This time his left leg snapped. In a swift move, Taylor grabbed the hyena's tail and for a moment it got distracted. Taylor held it firm. He had a Swiss knife with him. With one violent stroke he slashed it on the tail and backside of the hyena. The knife flew off but was enough to give a gash to the animal and it bolted ahead with pain, howling and screaming. The help had reached. The Toyota was standing parallel to the Land Rover. The hyenas had receded a large distance away amidst all the commotion. Carlos was brutally injured.

*   *   *

Carlos was gazing at the roof. The AC was purring away. The doctors had just left. Friends were around. He gazed at the plaster on his leg and bandage on his arm. The group was silent, stunned from the night's experience. Hearts were pounding but with relief. "What happened to the Land Rover? Why did it stop?" asked Tori angrily to James. Charles quietly said "We towed it back today. The fuel tank was empty. You should have checked before 'stealing it'." Tori felt sheepish. "I am sorry" she said. "Never take nature for granted. Remember you were in the home of the wild beasts and not vice versa. Only if you had heeded to the instructions. Anyway, all's well that ends well."

*   *   *

The airstrip: the morning after, as if
nothing happened last night

It took many years to cope with the traumatic experience. Many years later, they met at a reunion. Christina, Abdul and Richard, their college friends had also come. Christina said "Guys we are planning a trip to Africa for a wildlife safari. I have seen the wild animals in a zoo. I want to camp in the night in a national park and see some lions and shake hands or rather hand-paw shake, just like the Greek mythological hero Androceles." Carlos, Tori and Taylor froze.

8

I HAVE BEEN HERE BEFORE: MY HOUNDING PURSUIT

It was a dark lane, with an upslope. I could barely see ahead. The visibility was poor. There was a haze, some smoke and smell of burning charcoal. I was very lonely....I woke up with a start. I saw my mother lying by my side. She was warm, very warm. Her hair tresses were flickering on my face under the fan. I clung to her. I needed her. She hugged me back. I slept off.

I was three years then. That was when my father was posted in Assam. He used to work for the Oil and Natural Gas Commission (ONGC). My parents are very fond us, my brother and me. My father would first remove his office clothes and wash his hands after coming from his office. Next he would just catch hold of both of us and we would cuddle and play for a while before my mother would be laying out lunch. This was a daily affair. I would look forward to it. My natural body clock was fully synchronized with his arrival time and I would invariably be waiting at the main door for him.

He would be getting me lots of toys whenever he went away for a few days on a tour. And I would be breaking some of them on the very first day. He loved it. And he would get me more. We went out for picnics. I would accompany my elder brother to the school bus in the mornings and insist on going to school. I would also carry a school bag with my tiffin box; to drop my elder sibling to the bus stop. I would climb the bus and refuse to get down. Then after some coaxing I would oblige.

Then one day my mother admitted me to the preschool. I was really happy. I remember some months later I was sitting in the lap of my parents playing with alphabet blocks, learning the fun way. My mother announced dinner: my favorite grilled chicken with fruits. I chomped on the chicken and the fresh fruit salad. My mother put me to sleep and must have joined me some time later after winding up the house. I was in a dark lane, with an upslope. I could barely see ahead. The visibility was poor. There was a haze, some smoke and smell of burning charcoal. I saw a rickshaw. The man was lean. I could barely recognize the face. He was just behind me. The road was cobblestoned. I could smell the horse dung. The haze and smoke was over the road. It was cold. There were some distant lights. It was lonely, very, very lonely….I woke up terrified. My eyes met my mother's loving eyes. She had sensed it. "Anything wrong? Scared baby?" I just clutched at her with my chubby hands and put my arms around her. I slept off in peace.

Some years had passed by. I was eight now. A big boy. The nightmare had come once again but nothing to add in details. I was with my father in the market at Connaught place New Delhi. We were walking in the B block towards the A block. We turned within the B block and crossed over towards the Connaught circus end. It was around eight o clock. There was a small lane onto my right. I glanced at it. It was dark. There was no upslope. But there was a haze. I could smell the coal. I saw a lean man with menacing eyes looking at me. He was few meters away in the lane. I was holding my father's hand while walking. My walk must have slowed down. The lane was barely three meters across in width, which we were crossing. My father asked "all ok?" I looked to him on the left and said "Papa, look on the right, the visibility in the lane is poor and a man is standing there threatening me." He said "Where?" I looked to the right. There was nothing. The lane was normal. Few people were walking. No smoke. A bookseller, a newspaper vendor, and a chawariwala were selling chaat. It was reasonably well lighted. My father was puzzled. He said "You are probably tired. Let's go home. Have dinner and sleep." We moved on. I looked back again at the lane. It was empty, dark, hazy… The man was smiling wickedly. He had a steel knife in his hand!

I was disturbed. Next day I discussed with my parents. We could find no explanation. Yes it was true that I had been sleep deprived, the night before the 'daytime nightmare'. I had been watching movies late night with my cousins, being summer vacations.

Some time passed by. I was in class seven. It was the history class. The teacher was discussing the post British colonial era. We were studying the early years post independence. The chapter was on the partition of British India into India and Pakistan. I had already read the chapter twice before. I was sitting on the last bench. This hefty guy Hitesh was sitting in front of me. I took shelter in his size and probably dozed off. The cobblestone lane was dark and hazy. I could see a horse silhouette in the distance. Dark times. I was walking the upslope. I turned back and I could see my parents going off in a rickshaw. They told me to wait there. They said that they would be back soon. I could hear some wailing, crying, sloganeering of crowds. But the road was empty. I was walking to a nearby bench. I was very tired. I thought I should sit. But why did my parents leave me? There was killing going around on the streets of Delhi. India had been split. The year was 1948. But the riots had not stopped. There was a calendar lying on the road with May 1948 displayed. I turned around towards the upslope. The rickshaw was approaching. Those piercing eyes. Rest all haze. The smell of horse dung was strong in my nose. He indicated me to sit in the rickshaw.

It pained. The pain was severe. My cheeks were red and my back was aching. I opened my eyes. Our history teacher Mr Thapa was furious "How dare you sleep in my class?" He handed me another slap. "I am sorry sir" I said.

Why do I keep getting the same dream? What is the link? My mother said that it might have been related to my previous life experiences. She said that these were experiences of having lived in a past time with a different body and personality. The series of dreams had made me curious as to when and where my past life could have been. One thing was certain. It was around Delhi. Time was post independence. But where was this?

A year passed by. I was playing a tennis match with my friend at the tennis courts at the Delhi Gymkhana. There were some players waiting to play. There was a tall man, well built, sharp features. He was cheering me. My opponent was elder to me. Maybe a college student, he was stout, short and a good player. The game ended. We shook hands. He introduced himself as Aryan. The cheering guy came over to me and said, "Well played. Your game is good. My name is Harris. Will meet again. Bye." We bade goodbye and I went to the parking. My driver with the car was waiting. He opened the door. The Toyota Camry glided across the roads of Delhi. There was an unease. Harris and Aryan were appearing familiar. I had never met Harris before. He was friendly. But why was that? Aryan, I had met once before. We had played once earlier too. But they were too familiar and friendly just for an acquaintance. Maybe staying in an impersonal city like Delhi had made me too suspicious. Maybe people were really good. Greeting and smiling at strangers was perfectly normal in the West. But not in India. Here people view you with suspicion. I was thinking too much. Anyway I was extremely happy with the tennis match. My game had improved. I reached home. I rushed to the shower. Mom as usual had made a lovely dinner. Rajma and chawal, my favourite. I kissed my Mom goodnight and went off to sleep. I put an alarm for five in the morning. I had to study for the upcoming final exams.

There was a large brown building made of bricks and large glass windows with a large road in front of it. There was a huge red building on the opposite side of the road. Very huge. There was lane by the side of the brown building. It was dark. There was smoke and haze all around. I was sitting in the rickshaw. The rickshaw made a U turn and started moving upslope. I asked the rickshaw puller "Where are you taking me? My parents asked me to stay here." He said, "They have sent me to pick you up." Anyway I was just six years old. There is no way I could resist. So I continued. But I was puzzled. Why would my parents send him to take me? They had just left few minutes ago. When did they meet him? Why is he coming from the opposite direction? The rickshaw reached a small diversion and turned left and stopped. The rickshaw puller got down. He held me by my shoulder and pulled me. I heard voices. I turned behind and my parents were standing some distance away. The rickshaw puller pulled a steel knife and put to my neck. He asked my parents for ten rupees. "I need to feed my family. The riots have destroyed my house. My family is on roads. I don't care what religion you are from. I need money." There are two more people with my parents. The faces are familiar. Very familiar. My father put his hand into his handbang. "Don't! Don't act smart. I will kill your son!" "But I am taking out the money. It is in the purse in my handbag." My father opened the bag. The first thing that came out of the bag was a shawl and then a small dagger and then a purse. I remember him saying to my mother, "times are bad. We should keep it with us always. We never know when it might be useful." The rickshaw puller screamed when he saw the dagger. He raised the steel knife. I saw his face in the streetlight perhaps for the last time. He had piercing narrow eyes, grey beard, narrow forehead and a long neck. The two familiar people and my parents rushed towards me. But with one swift movement the knife sliced my throat. I could see my body lying in a pool of blood. I was a few meters above the body around the height of the streetlight pole. The rickshaw puller had disappeared in to the dark lane. The familiar people and my parents were wailing.

I got up. It was about two in the morning. The dream was bad. But it had reached finality. If it was a past life, then now I knew how it had ended. I had been killed for ten rupees. Ten rupees was a large sum in those days. But now I recollected the familiar faces. They were Harris and Aryan! How could that be? Maybe because I had met them the same evening and it was a pleasant meeting, so I must have remembered them. That was the explanation I gave myself.

All went normal thereafter. I went to the Gymkhana few times after my exams. However I never met Aryan or Harris. We moved to Mussourie sometime later. Many years passed by. I was in class twelve now. No more dreams. Life was peaceful. The year was 2011. I had gone to my grandfather's place for his cataract surgery along with my father for a couple of days to Pune. Grandpa was well now. We took the Air India Pune Delhi flight in the evening back home. The flight landed on time at the swanky T3 terminal New Delhi. After an enjoyable walk on the walkalator we moved on. We collected our baggage and headed for the airport metro station. It was life as usual. The Metro glided into the station and then smoothly it went off. We got down at New Delhi Metro station and started moving up the escalators towards the exit towards the New Delhi railway station. We had to board the Nanda Devi Express onwards to Dehradun and would take a taxi to Mussourie from there.

We got out of the exit door from the Metro station. There it was! I held my father's hand. "Dad, I have been here before!" I said. "No son. Never. I have been here before, but I have got you here for the first time" said my father. "No, no. I was here. Look at the huge large red building in front. The New Delhi Railway station!" I said. "So? That picture is pasted all over Google. You must have seen it there" said my father. "No, no you are not getting it. It is the same place I have been seeing in my dreams!" We stood still. My father froze. We were looking straight at the red railway station building. We had to take a few steps, about 25 meters to the right of the exit to cross the main road, as the front of the Metro exit was barricaded. I said, "There is a lane to the right side of this Metro building which joins the main road which we are seeing straight ahead and the lane goes slightly upslope on the opposite end. The lane is dimly lighted and there is a diversion into two lanes some hundred meters ahead. The right turn is sharper and the left is gentler." My father was dumbfounded and so was I. My heart was pounding faster. We turned right from the Metro exit. Walked some 25 meters and sure enough the dark lane was there! It was dimly lighted, with a slight upslope and exactly with the same diversion as I had seen in my nightmares. What was happening? I thought that a closure report on my nightmare had been filed by my mind some years ago. Why was I being taken by fate to an actual place which I had seen and remembered so vividly? What was life up to? I am not interested in my past life. I want to live the present one. Neither Dad nor I was interested in 'walking up the dark memory lane'. I had already told them about the details of the nightmare. With the 'final closure filed by fate' today I was relieved that now it will be over at last. Now I had seen everything including the place where I ended my previous life. I was at happy, sad, fearful and satisfied all at the same time.

Anyway we turned left towards the railway station. We had two small strolley bags and a handbag. We heard a voice. A rickshaw puller, "Sahib, do you want a rickshaw to the station?" We were tired. I said yes. We put our stuff on it and sat on the narrow seats. "How much will you charge?" I asked. "Fifty rupees" he said. "I never haggle with rickshaw pullers and vegetable vendors. You people are hard working and poor. But it is always good to fix the price beforehand" I said. The rickshaw puller nodded. We crossed the main road. We entered the parking lot of the railway station. He got down and pulled the rickshaw manually as he could not cycle because of the slow speed and some upslope. We reached the station in next two minutes. I got the bags down. My father gave him a fifty rupee note and another twenty rupees extra. He was visibly pleased. "Thank you Sahib. I need to feed my family. The riots in Muzzafarnagar last year have destroyed my house. My family is on roads" the rickshaw puller said. I looked up. He had piercing narrow eyes, grey beard, narrow forehead and a long neck! Same face as in my dreams, the guy who had killed me in my previous life, if I can say so. But his face was calm and happy. My head was in a tizzy. What was happening? Will this never end? My father didn't understand. We turned back and started towards the baggage X ray machine. The rickshaw puller had disappeared from the view. I wanted to leave this area of New Delhi railway station- Metro station-dark lane complex as fast as possible. How can the rickshaw puller be alive after 63 years? And still looking the same age and doing the same job at the same location? Is he a ghost? Or is he Count Dracula from Austria?

We heard a loud commotion. It was all happening about 50 meters behind us. We turned back. A rickshaw was lying turtle. Mr. Dracula was lying on the road. He was dead. A small purse, a bed sheet and a rusted steel knife had fallen out of the belongings box of the rickshaw. An SUV had hit him over. The SUV owners were standing next to him along with the police. The scene had also been captured on the CCTV. It was most likely the rickshaw puller's fault. He was riding the rickshaw on the wrong side in a one way road and had come out of the shadow of a truck. I recognized the SUV owner and the co driver. Harris and Aryan! The police was busy questioning them. I made no attempts to meet them. I was too scared and troubled by the evening's turn of

New Delhi railway station: I was being
haunted with all the day's happenings

events. As I turned back both Harris's and Aryan's eyes
met mine. They probably never recognized me. We might
have missed our train. So we turned around and made our
way to the platform. Our train was lined up at platform
number 14. We quietly boarded the train. My father had
not heard yet from me about the rickshaw puller, Harris
and Aryan. He only knew the story till we last came out
of the Metro station. He had gooseflesh when I told him
the entire story.

A year later, I went to Delhi Gymkhana. I thought
that I should find out about Aryan and Harris and meet
them. For what? I didn't know. Anyway I went to the
secretary's office. I showed my membership to the clerk.
Now here comes the biggest mystery... There was nobody
by this name registered as a member or guest in the last
seven years! I checked the computer entries on the day
I played tennis. There were five entries in my name. So

it was not difficult to check the dates for the entries for Harris or Aryan. Then who were Harris and Aryan? They tried to save me in my previous life unsuccessfully but avenged my death now with an exact replica of the man who killed me sixty-three years ago at almost the same place where it happened. How come there was a rusted steel knife alongside Dracula, similar to what I seen in my dreams? Why did Harris say 'Will meet again? Bye' when I met him at the tennis court last? Has the nightmare ended? Will it come back again? I think there are no loose ends left. But I have thought so on many previous occasions too. The only quantum of solace is that nothing related to the nightmare or the people associated with it have repeated their presence in my life again. It is 2016 now. Or was it all a saga of premonitions? One will never know.

Good night. Wish me luck. No more nightmares!